THE SMALL ADVENTURE
OF POPEYE AND ELVIS

Also by Barbara O'Connor

Beethoven in Paradise
Me and Rupert Goody
Moonpie and Ivy
Fame and Glory in Freedom, Georgia
Taking Care of Moses
How to Steal a Dog
Greetings from Nowhere

BARBARA O'CONNOR

SQUARE
FISH

FARRAR STRAUS GIROUX
NEW YORK

Special thanks to Ben,
the original Yoo-hoo boat maker

SQUARE
FISH

An Imprint of Macmillan

Library of Congress Cataloging-in-Publication Data
O'Connor, Barbara.
The small adventure of Popeye and Elvis / Barbara O'Connor.
   p.   cm.
Summary: In Fayette, South Carolina, the highlight of Popeye's summer is
learning vocabulary words with his grandmother until a motorhome gets
stuck nearby and Elvis, the oldest boy living inside, joins Popeye in finding
the source of strange boats floating down the creek.
ISBN: 978-0-312-65932-5
[1. Friendship—Fiction.   2. Adventure and adventurers—Fiction.
3. Recreational vehicles—Fiction.   4. Grandmothers—Fiction   5. Dogs—
Fiction.   6. South Carolina—Fiction.]   I. Title.

PZ7.0217SMC 2009
[Fic]—dc22

                                                        2008024145

Originally published in the United States by Frances Foster Books,
an imprint of Farrar Straus Giroux
First Square Fish Edition: January 2011
Square Fish logo designed by Filomena Tuosto
Book design by Irene Metaxatos
www.squarefishbooks.com

10   9   8   7   6   5   4   3   2   1

LEXILE 750L

To Willy and Grady,
who have shared so many
small adventures with me

THE SMALL ADVENTURE
OF POPEYE AND ELVIS

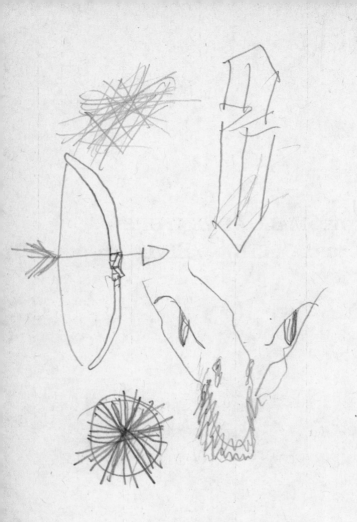

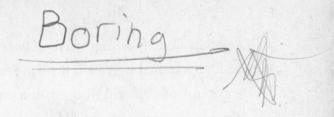
1

DRIP.

Drip.

Drip.

Popeye opened his eye and looked up at the heart-shaped stain on the ceiling of his bedroom. Rusty water squeezed out of the hole in the peeling plaster and dropped onto the foot of his bed.

Drip.

Drip.

Drip.

It had been raining for over a week.

All day.

Every day.

The stain on the ceiling used to be a tiny circle. Popeye had watched it grow a little more each day.

He got out of bed and nudged Boo with his foot. The old dog lifted his head and looked up at Popeye, his sagging skin drooping down over his sad, watery eyes.

"Still raining," Popeye said.

Boo's big, heavy head flopped back down on the floor, and he let out a long, low dog groan.

Popeye padded across the cracked linoleum floor of the hallway and into the bathroom. He splashed water on his face and ran his wet fingers over his head. The stubble of his new summer buzz cut felt scratchy, like a cat's tongue. His white scalp showed through his pale blond hair.

He examined his teeth in the mirror.

They looked clean.

He rubbed his good eye.

Then he rubbed his bad eye. The one that was always squinted shut thanks to his uncle Dooley.

Popeye hadn't always been Popeye. Before he was three years old, he had been Henry.

But when he was three, his uncle Dooley had

placed a small green crab apple on the fence post out back and turned to his girlfriend and said, "Watch this, Charlene."

Then he had walked back twenty paces, like a gunslinger, taken aim with his Red Ryder BB gun, and pulled the trigger.

Dooley was not a very good aim.

Charlene was not impressed.

When the BB hit Henry square in the eye, she had screamed bloody murder and carried on so much that when Popeye's grandmother, Velma, came running out of the house to see what all the fuss was about, she had thought it was Charlene who'd been shot in the eye.

Popeye had been Popeye ever since.

And Charlene was long gone. (Which hadn't bothered Dooley one little bit 'cause there were plenty more where she came from.)

Popeye went up the hall to the kitchen, his bare feet stirring up little puffs of dust on the floor. Velma didn't care much about keeping a clean house. She mainly cared about not cracking up.

"You get old, you crack up," she told Popeye

when she couldn't find her reading glasses or opened the closet door and forgot why.

While Popeye made toast with powdered sugar on top, Velma sat at the kitchen table with her eyes closed, reciting the kings and queens of England in chronological order.

"Edward V, Richard III, Henry VII, Henry VIII, Edward VI, Mary I . . ."

Popeye knew that when she got to the last one, Elizabeth II, she would probably start all over again.

"Egbert, Ethelwulf, Ethelbald, Ethelbert . . ."

Reciting the kings and queens of England in chronological order was exercising Velma's brain and keeping her from cracking up.

But sometimes, Popeye worried that it wasn't working.

This was a big worry.

Popeye needed Velma to not crack up because no one else in his family was very good at taking care of things.

Not his father, who lived up in Chattanooga and sold smoke-damaged rugs out of the back of a pickup truck.

Not his mother, who came and went but never

told anybody where she came from or where she went to.

And definitely not his uncle Dooley, who lived in a rusty trailer in the backyard and sometimes worked at the meatpacking plant and sometimes sold aluminum siding and sometimes watched TV all day.

Popeye's grandmother, Velma, was the only one good at taking care of things.

"Edward VIII, George VI, Elizabeth II." Velma opened her eyes. Instead of starting all over again with Egbert, she shuffled over to the kitchen counter and poured herself a cup of coffee.

"Hey there, burrhead," she said, running her hand over Popeye's fuzzy buzz cut.

"Hey."

"What're you gonna do today?"

Popeye shrugged.

"This dern rain is driving me nuts," she said, stirring a heaping spoonful of sugar into her coffee.

Popeye stared out at the muddy yard. A waterfall of rust-colored rainwater poured off the edge of the metal roof of the shed out back and made a river. The river snaked its way down the gravel driveway and into the drainage ditch that ran along the side of the road. The ditch was nearly overflowing. Every now and then, soda cans or plastic bags floated by in front of the house.

Boo ambled into the kitchen and ate a scrap of toast off the floor under the table, his tail wagging in slow motion.

Back . . .

And forth.

Back . . .

And forth.

Popeye licked powdered sugar off his fingers and went into the living room.

Dooley was stretched out on the couch, snoring one of those throat-gurgling kinds of snores. The smell of cigarettes hovered in the air around him and clung to the worn corduroy couch.

Popeye flopped into Velma's big armchair. The metal tray table beside it was stacked with crossword puzzle magazines. Crossword puzzles were good brain exercises, too. Velma knew more words than anybody. She taught Popeye one new word every week. He wrote it on the patio with sidewalk chalk and studied it until it got smudged up by Dooley's worn-out work boots or washed away by the rain.

This week's word was *vicissitude*, but he hadn't been able to write it on the patio yet because of the rain.

vicissitude: *noun*; a change of circumstances, typically one that is unwelcome or unpleasant

Popeye slouched down in the chair and slapped his bare foot on the floor.

Slap.

Slap.

He looked out the window, wishing that maybe some vicissitude would come along and make this dern rain stop. Even something unwelcome or unpleasant would probably be better than this.

He watched a fly land on Dooley's big toe.

He wrote *vicissitude* with his finger on the flowered fabric of Velma's chair.

He scooped saltine cracker crumbs off the coffee table and tossed them over to Boo, who had settled onto his raggedy quilt by the woodstove.

The hands of the clock over the couch jerked noisily.

Tick. Tick. Tick.

Around and around.

Tick. Tick. Tick.

Popeye was beginning to hate that clock. He was sick to high heaven of watching it turn minutes into hours and hours into days.

Every day the same.

So *what* if the rain stopped? Popeye thought.

It would still be boring.

It would always be boring in Fayette, South Carolina.

Every day would always be the same.

Popeye was certain about that.

But Popeye was wrong.

Because that very day, that day with the rain dripping out of the heart-shaped stain on the ceiling and that fly sitting there on Dooley's big toe, things changed.

Elvis came to town.

2

POPEYE PUSHED the screen door open and went out on the porch.

The rain had stopped.

Finally.

The dark clouds were drifting apart, and a sliver of sun poked through, making the raindrops glisten on the leathery leaves of the magnolia tree out front.

The water in the rainspout still made gurgling noises, but the little river snaking down the driveway was slowing down and spreading into puddles.

Popeye jumped off the rickety wooden porch, sending up a spray of muddy water. He went out to the road and walked along the edge of the drainage ditch. Every now and then, he picked up a few pieces of gravel and tossed them into the murky water.

Plunk.

Plunk.

Plunk.

Boo ambled along behind him, his head hanging so low his floppy ears dragged on the wet gravel.

Then Popeye rounded the curve in the road, and right there in front of him was the last thing he would ever have expected to see.

A motor home.

A *big* motor home.

Big as a house.

Almost.

It tilted precariously to the side, one of its giant wheels sunk deep down into the gloppy red mud of the road.

"Dang, Boo," Popeye said. "Wouldya look at that!"

The lopsided motor home sparkled like tinfoil in the sun. Glittery gold lightning bolts zigzagged along its sides. On the front, under the enormous windshield, was a painting of a coyote, howling up at a round yellow moon.

Bumper stickers and decals were stuck every which way all over it. Above the door. Along the roof.

SEE ROCK CITY

CAN'T DRIVE IN THE RAIN?
GO BACK TO CALIFORNIA.

I ATE CATFISH AT COUNTRY BILL'S
ON HIGHWAY 14

American flags and smiley faces and peace symbols bordered the curtain-covered windows.

Just looking at that big silver motor home was pure entertainment.

Popeye wondered if there was anybody inside it. He put his ear up against the side and listened.

Silence.

He walked around behind it. Beat-up bicycles of every size were tied to a rack with bright orange rope. A narrow metal ladder led up to the roof.

Popeye stood on his tiptoes, trying to see what was up there, but it was too high. Maybe he could climb up that little ladder and just take a quick peek.

Popeye looked up the road.

Then he looked down the road.

He looked at Boo. "Tell me if anybody comes," he said.

His heart raced as he climbed up the ladder and peered over the top. Aluminum lawn chairs and a rusty barbecue grill were strapped to the railing that ran along the sides.

Popeye looked up the road.

Then he looked down the road.

Then he crawled out onto the top of the motor home and stood up, his knees shaking and his stomach fluttering.

In one corner was a big metal toolbox. Popeye tiptoed over and opened it. Inside were footballs and baseballs and badminton rackets. Jump ropes and Frisbees and croquet mallets. A pair of stilts. A pogo stick.

"Hey, you skinny-headed ding-dong!"

Popeye let the lid of the toolbox slam shut with a clang.

"You want me to come up there and give you a knuckle sandwich for lunch?"

Popeye peered over the edge of the roof. A whole

passel of scruffy-looking kids glared up at him. The oldest one stood in front of the others with his fists jammed into his waist. His hair was long. Dark, wavy curls flopped over his eyes and covered his ears.

Popeye didn't know what to do.

A couple of the kids gathered around Boo, hugging him, stroking his back, lifting his ears.

Popeye felt a little irritated at Boo for not warning him about these kids.

"I was just looking," he said, his voice coming out all trembly.

"You wanna look at something, you come down here and look at this." The boy shook his fist at Popeye.

"Yeah," one of the other boys said. "You come down here and look at *that*."

"This your dog?" the only girl in the bunch said. She kissed Boo right on the mouth and hugged his neck. A wild halo of curls bounced around her head, like little springs.

Popeye nodded. "His name is Boo."

The smallest boy kept saying, "Shake," and holding his grubby hand out for Boo to shake hands with him.

Boo was not interested.

"What kinda dog is he?" the boy asked.

"Oh," Popeye said, trying hard to make his trembly voice sound cool and casual-like, "Part this, part that, and part the other thing." That was Velma's line, but Popeye figured some humor was called for now. He grinned at the kids, hoping to calm things down a little with that oldest boy still glaring up at him.

Popeye glanced from kid to kid. They all had the same curly hair. The same dark eyes. The same skinny legs all covered with scabs and mosquito bites. The boys were barefoot and shirtless, their shoulders sunburned and freckled. The girl wore a camouflage T-shirt over a bathing suit and tap shoes. Black tap shoes tied with yellow ribbon and covered with mud.

"Get yourself on down here," the glaring boy said, his fists still jammed into his waist.

Popeye put one foot onto the ladder.

Then he put the other foot onto the ladder.

And then he went down.

Down.

Down.

3

"WHAT HAPPENED to your eye?" one of the boys said.

"My uncle, Dooley, shot it with a BB gun."

The boys looked at each other with eye-widened, jaw-dropping glee and said, "Cool!" and "Awesome!" but the girl said, "Eeeyew!"

"Turn your pockets inside out," the oldest boy said. The other kids gathered in a bunch behind him.

"What for?" Popeye said.

"We got checkers and stuff up there." The boy jerked his head toward the roof of the motor home.

"Yeah, and some good rocks," one of the other boys said.

The girl squinted at him. "Did you take our good rocks?" she said.

Popeye turned the pockets of his shorts inside out. Two quarters and a Tootsie Roll fell onto the wet gravel.

The girl darted over and snatched the Tootsie Roll.

"You can have it," Popeye said, picking up the quarters.

"It's all mushy," she said, tossing the gooey candy into the drainage ditch.

It made a *ploink* noise and disappeared beneath the muddy water.

"What were you doing up there, anyways?" the oldest boy said.

Popeye shrugged. "Just looking."

"Ain't you ever seen a motor home before?"

"Not one like that." Popeye looked over at the shiny, tilted motor home. "At least, not up close," he added.

"It's a Holiday Rambler," the boy said.

A Holiday Rambler?

Popeye loved the sound of that. "You on vacation?" he asked.

"Heck, no," the boy said. "That's where we live."

"All the time?"

The boy nodded. "All the time."

Popeye had never heard anything so glorious. This gang of scruffy kids *lived* in that silver motor home with the howling coyote and the lightning bolts.

"Why'd you come to Fayette?" he said.

Elvis shrugged. "Took a wrong turn."

"Where'd you come from?"

"Come from all over."

Popeye remembered one of Velma's vocabulary words.

nomad: *noun*; a wanderer

Popeye tried to imagine being a nomad in a Holiday Rambler instead of waking up every livelong day in the same old place where nothing ever happened.

"You wanna be in our club?" the girl asked.

The boy whirled around and yelled, *"I'm* the inviter of this club!" He punched her in the arm with a knuckle, making her jump around and holler.

Loud.

When she was done hollering, she kicked him in the shin with the metal toe of her tap shoe.

Then they scuffled around in the gravel road for a bit, calling each other names and yanking hair until the girl held her arms up in the air and made peace signs and hollered, "Truce!"

The boy turned to Popeye. "You wanna be in our club?" he said.

"What club?"

"The Spit and Swear Club."

"What's that?"

"A club where you spit and swear," the boy said, tossing his head back and spitting in the ditch.

All of the other kids spat in the ditch.

Popeye spat in the ditch.

Then the boy let loose with a string of the most amazing and wonderful swearwords, and all the other kids did the same until the air was filled with the swearingest words Popeye had ever heard. He had always thought his uncle Dooley was pretty good at swearing, but these kids made Dooley look like a harp-strumming angel.

So Popeye joined in, calling swearwords out into the steamy air beside the ditch.

That seemed to please the oldest boy. He looked solemnly at Popeye and said, "Okay, you can be in our club."

Then he pointed at the other kids one by one. "Calvin, Prissy, Walter, Willis, Shorty." He jabbed a thumb at himself and said, "Elvis."

Popeye jabbed a thumb at himself and said, "Popeye."

All the kids started hooting and hollering and poking each other with their elbows and holding their sides and saying, *"Popeye?"*

Popeye's face grew hot.

Elvis ignored the other kids and slapped a hand on Popeye's shoulder. "I'm making you senior vice president," he said.

"Hey!" Calvin hollered. "*I'm* senior vice president."

"Not anymore, you ain't," Elvis said.

Calvin clamped his mouth shut tight and glared at Elvis.

Popeye didn't want to make Calvin any madder

than he already was, so he tried hard to keep his face serious and not all smiley like he was feeling inside.

He had started this day as a fly-staring, clock-watching, bored boy.

And now here he was, senior vice president of the Spit and Swear Club.

4

POPEYE SAT on the side of the road and waited. The door of the motor home stayed shut. The curtains stayed drawn. No sounds came from inside.

"Guess it's too early," he said to Boo.

Boo's tail brushed back and forth in the weeds, still damp with the morning dew.

Popeye wanted to see inside that motor home more than anything.

The day before, right after he had become senior vice president of the Spit and Swear Club, a window of the motor home had slid open and a woman had called out, "Y'all get on in here," and all those kids had gone tumbling inside without so much as a goodbye, leaving Popeye to spend the rest of the day alone.

Bored.

Again.

So first thing this morning he had dashed out to wait.

"What in the name of sweet Bernice in heaven is *that*?"

Popeye looked up to see his uncle Dooley strolling down the road toward him. Dooley hadn't seen the stuck-in-the-mud motor home yet. He had slept on the couch all day yesterday and then tried to get his car started about a million times before he gave up and went out back to his trailer to sleep some more.

"It's a Holiday Rambler," Popeye said.

Dooley took his baseball cap off, scratched his head, and let out a whistle. "That thing is some kinda stuck," he said, examining the big tire sunk deep in the mud.

"Yep." Popeye looked over at the leaning motor home. "It's a vicissitude," he said, "getting stuck in the mud like that."

Dooley probably didn't have much to say about a vicissitude, so he said, "Anybody in there?"

"Yep."

"Who?"

"A bunch of kids," Popeye said. "They live in there."

Just then a rattletrap of a car came bouncing down the road and jerked to a stop beside them, sending out a spray of dirt and gravel. Dooley said, "See ya," and climbed in the backseat with a couple of other guys, and the car drove off, leaving a trail of black smoke behind it.

The door of the motor home swung open with a bang. Elvis stomped down the step and walked right past Popeye with his fists jammed into his pockets and his hair flopping over his eyes.

Popeye jumped up. "Where you going?"

Elvis glanced at him and kept going, right up the middle of the road.

Walter (or maybe it was Willis) hollered from a window of the motor home, "Mama said you better get back here!"

Elvis shook his fist in the air.

Every now and then he hauled off and kicked a piece of gravel so hard he made an *oomph* noise.

"What's wrong?" Popeye hurried along beside

him. Boo trotted behind them with his tongue hanging out, panting.

"Calvin is a hog-stinkin' sack of nothin'," Elvis said.

A hog-stinkin' sack of nothin'?

That was as good an insult as Popeye had heard in a long time. He made a mental note to remember it.

"How come?" Popeye said.

"He's just a toe-jam tattletale, that's all."

A toe-jam tattletale?

That was another good one worth remembering.

"How come?" Popeye asked again.

Elvis stopped suddenly and whirled around to face Popeye. "Let's do something," he said.

"Like what?"

"I don't know," Elvis said. "What's there to do around here?"

Popeye looked around.

Weeds. Ditch. Trees. Mailbox. House. Shed. Trailer.

He shrugged. "Not much."

Elvis kicked at a rusty can on the side of the road, sending it tumbling into the weeds. "Shoot," he said. "Must be *something* to do."

"What about the Spit and Swear Club?" Popeye asked. He was dying to do some more spitting and swearing.

"Aw, that stupid club ain't a club no more," Elvis said.

Popeye's heart sank clear down to his sneakers. "How come?"

" 'Cause it was stupid."

Popeye could hardly believe his days as senior vice president of the best club he'd ever been in—shoot, the *only* club he'd ever been in—were already over.

Poof! Just like that.

When they got to the corner, where the road met the main highway, Elvis scooped up a handful of gravel and hurled it at the stop sign.

Thwang.

Popeye scooped up some gravel and threw it at the stop sign, too.

Thwang.

They walked along the shoulder of the highway for a while. Popeye liked the way Elvis didn't want to talk all the time like most other kids did.

Every once in a while, they stopped to pick some

blackberries. They caught grasshoppers. They found a soggy lottery ticket in the weeds. They stopped to poke at a snapping turtle sunning on the hot asphalt at the edge of the road. Popeye used a stick, but not Elvis. Elvis poked that nasty looking snapping turtle with his finger. Quick, hard jabs that made the turtle yank its head into its shell with a hiss.

After a while, they turned around and went back to Popeye's house and sat on the porch steps. Velma's voice drifted through the screen door from inside the house.

"George IV, William IV, Victoria, Edward VII . . ."

Popeye hoped Elvis wouldn't think Velma was cracking up. But Elvis acted like it was the most normal thing in the world for some old lady to be reciting the kings and queens of England in chronological order.

The boys watched a dragonfly flit around the weeds out by the mailbox.

They played tic-tac-toe in the dirt with a stick.

They took turns scratching Boo's stomach with the tic-tac-toe stick.

Then, out of the clear blue, Elvis grabbed Popeye

by the shoulders and gave him a little shake. "Let's have an adventure," he said.

Popeye blinked. "An adventure?"

Elvis nodded. "It doesn't have to be a *big* adventure," Elvis said. "It can be a small adventure." He gave Popeye another little shake. "Let's have a *small* adventure."

A small adventure!

That was exactly what Popeye had been needing. A small adventure.

"Okay," he said.

Elvis ran off toward the woods behind the shed. "Come on!" he called to Popeye over his shoulder.

Popeye jumped off the porch steps.

"Come on, Boo," he said. "Let's go have a small adventure." Then he hurried after Elvis, his stomach turning flips of excitement and his heart light and breezy as a cloud.

5

POPEYE AND ELVIS spent all afternoon trying to have a small adventure.

They followed a trail that ran through the woods and ended up at a dirt road.

They followed the dirt road until it came to a dead end.

They overturned moss-covered rocks in the creek behind Popeye's house and built a dam out of branches and mud to trap minnows.

They walked to the gas station down on the main highway, where Popeye was never supposed to go without asking Velma first.

But they didn't have an adventure.

Not even a small one.

"This place is boring," Elvis said, dragging a stick through the dirt on the side of the highway as they made their way back to Popeye's house.

"Yeah, I know." Popeye dragged a stick in the dirt, too.

Boo sauntered along behind them, stopping from time to time to sniff a signpost or scratch a flea.

"Maybe we should start the Spit and Swear Club again," Popeye said, trying to sound like he didn't care one bit, even though he was about to bust wide open from hoping.

"Naw." Elvis shook his head. "We'd have to let Calvin join, and you know what he is."

Popeye's hope popped like a balloon and disappeared into the sultry summer air. "Yeah," he said. "A hog-stinkin' sack of nothin'."

"Dern right." Elvis sliced the air with his stick in a big Z shape.

Zip.

Zip.

Zip.

"And a toe-jam tattletale," Popeye said.

"Dern right."

When they turned onto the gravel road, all those curly-haired kids came racing toward them.

Prissy and Calvin and Walter and Willis and Shorty.

"Daddy was digging and digging, but that wheel is stuck like cement and he's mad as fire and gone off somewhere," Walter said.

"And Mama don't even care," Prissy said, running over to give Boo a hug.

"Yeah," Shorty said. "She's just sittin' there cuttin' pictures out of the *Good Housekeeping* magazine." A line of grape Popsicle juice ran down his chin, his neck, and clear on down his stomach.

Elvis kept on walking like those kids were invisible. Popeye hurried after him.

"Where y'all going?" Prissy called, racing to catch up with them. She poked Elvis in the arm. "Where y'all going?" she repeated.

"None of your beeswax, bug-brain booger-breath," Elvis said.

Popeye grinned and walked beside Elvis like he knew where they were going.

That Elvis. He was for sure the best insulter Pop-eye had ever laid eyes on. No doubt about it.

The whole gang of them made their way down the side of the road, Popeye and Elvis walking silently, their hands jammed in their pockets, and all the others skipping along behind them, jibbering and jabbering, throwing rocks and picking wild-flowers and whistling for Boo to follow them.

Popeye couldn't help but notice how different Elvis was from all the others.

Elvis was taciturn.

taciturn: *adjective*; reserved or uncommunicative in speech; saying little

All the others were loquacious.

loquacious: *adjective*; talkative

Every now and then, Elvis jumped to the other side of the drainage ditch and back again.

Popeye jumped to the other side of the drainage ditch and back again.

All the others (except Shorty) jumped to the other side of the drainage ditch and back again.

After three or four good jumps, Prissy slipped in the mud and fell into the knee-deep water.

Elvis kept right on walking in that silent way of his, but all his brothers hooted and hollered, clutching their stomachs and slapping their knees. Prissy let loose with a string of cusswords and threw gravel at everybody before she sat on the side of the road to dump muddy water out of her tap shoes.

Then she ran off toward the motor home, promising to tell their mama on every one of them and threatening to eat all their M&M's.

When they got to Popeye's house, Elvis whipped around and yelled, "Y'all go on home and I mean it."

Walter looked at Willis and Willis looked at Calvin and Calvin nudged Shorty and they all raced off and disappeared around the curve in the road.

"Let's go check our minnow trap," Elvis said.

So Popeye and Elvis and Boo trotted through the weeds and jumped over logs and ducked under branches until they got to the creek.

The cool, clear water flowed through tree roots and tumbled over mossy rocks, settling into a pool formed by the dam of branches and mud the boys had built. About a dozen tiny silvery minnows darted around in the pool.

Elvis cupped his hands and scooped some up.

Popeye cupped his hands and scooped some up.

Elvis put his hands in the creek and let the minnows swim away.

Popeye put his hands in the creek and let the minnows swim away.

Then they sat on the mossy bank beside the creek.

The birds chirped above them.

The water gurgled below them.

Boo snored beside them.

And then . . .

. . . a small adventure came floating down the creek.

6

ELVIS JUMPED UP. "What's that?" he said.

Popeye leaned forward so he could get a better look at whatever it was floating toward them.

A tiny boat!

A yellow and brown and blue boat that dipped and bobbed as it made its way down the creek, bumping into rotten leaves that floated on the water and gliding smoothly over tiny waterfalls that flowed over the slippery rocks.

Popeye felt a swirl of excitement as the boat got closer.

A boat!

He had played in this creek about a bajillion times and had never, not once, seen a boat.

Elvis didn't even take his sneakers off before stepping down into the water to scoop it up. Then he climbed back onto the sloping creek bank, holding the little boat out in the palm of his hand.

Popeye peered at it with his good eye. "A Yoo-hoo box!" he said.

The boat was made out of a waxy cardboard Yoo-hoo chocolate drink box. Someone had made the box into a perfect boat, without a single piece of tape or staples to hold it together.

"I wonder where it came from," Popeye said.

Elvis looked up the creek. "Where does this creek start?"

Popeye lifted his shoulders and let them drop. "I've been a pretty far ways up there," he said, "but I've never been to the end."

"How far'd you go?"

"Not that far, I don't reckon." Popeye didn't want to tell Elvis that Velma wouldn't allow him to go farther than hollering distance from home.

Elvis peered inside the boat. "Hey!" he hollered. "There's something in here!"

He pulled out a tiny square of folded paper.

Popeye hopped from foot to foot while he watched Elvis unfold the paper.

Once.

Twice.

Three times.

Then he peered over Elvis's shoulder and both boys read out loud together:

"Yoo-hoo! Ha! Ha!"

Elvis looked at Popeye and Popeye looked at Elvis.

"What the heck kind of dang ignoramus talking is that?" Elvis said.

But Popeye's heart was thumping in his chest, and he felt an odd surge of love for the person who had written the note and sent it down the creek in that perfect little boat.

Well, maybe not love.

But *like*.

Popeye *liked* the person who had sent the note down the creek in the Yoo-hoo box.

He studied the note in Elvis's hand. The words were scrawled in big, sloppy letters with a blue colored pencil.

"Serendipity," he said.

Elvis's eyebrows squeezed together, and he frowned at Popeye. "What are you talking about?"

"Serendipity," Popeye repeated. "It's like when something good happens all of a sudden when you're not expecting it."

Serendipity had been last week's word from Velma, so Popeye knew all about it.

serendipity: *noun;* the occurrence of events by chance in a happy way

Elvis nodded. "Yeah."

They both leaned over and looked up the creek.

Popeye tried to imagine who in the world had sent that little Yoo-hoo boat down the creek.

Elvis brushed his hair out of his face and looked

at Popeye with narrowed, serious eyes. "We got to find out who sent this boat," he said.

Popeye nodded solemnly.

"Let's hide it," Elvis said.

The boys raked up a pile of rotten leaves with their hands. Elvis placed the boat on the ground beneath a crooked oak tree and they pushed the leaves over it, covering it completely.

"We got to keep this a secret from Calvin and them," Elvis said.

A little tingle of excitement ran through Popeye. He and Elvis had a *secret*!

As they made their way back down the path through the woods toward the field, Popeye called out, "Hey, Elvis, is this our small adventure?"

But Elvis just kept on walking in that way of his—head down, fists jammed in his pockets. Taciturn.

So Popeye turned to Boo and whispered, "Boo, I think this might be our small adventure."

7

EDWARD III, RICHARD II, Henry IV, Henry V . . .

Popeye ate cereal at the kitchen table while Velma tried to keep from cracking up.

When she got to Elizabeth II, Popeye said, "Me and Elvis are gonna be back yonder at the creek today, okay?"

Velma pulled a couple of squishy pink curlers out of her hair and tossed them into the fruit bowl on the table. "Don't you be going too far into them woods, you hear?" she said.

"Yes, ma'am."

"There's snakes and I don't know what else back there."

"Yes, ma'am."

"And you keep your eye on that boy Elvis," Velma said. "We don't know nothing about them people."

"Yes, ma'am."

"Seems to me like they oughta be gettin' that big ole trailer out of here, if you ask me."

"It's a Holiday Rambler."

Velma ran her fingers through her thin gray hair. "Who in the world ever heard of folks living like that, anyway? Them kids wouldn't be so wild if they lived in a house like normal folks." She shook her head and made a *tsk-tsk* noise. "Running around here like a pack of stray dogs."

Popeye put his cereal bowl in the sink and said, "They *like* living in a Holiday Rambler."

Velma made a little *pffft* sound and flapped her hand at Popeye. She shuffled across the floor in her ratty old slippers and poured herself another cup of coffee. "Maybe if Dooley'd get off his dern lazy behind and help those people, they could get that contraption out of here and be on their way."

Popeye felt a little knot growing in his stomach at the thought of the Holiday Rambler driving away with Elvis and all those kids inside, leaving a big empty space in the road and a whole summer full of boredom ahead.

"Come on, Boo," he called, and hurried out the front door. He hopped down the steps and raced to the silver motor home. The shiny gold lightning bolts on the side glittered in the morning sun.

He stood on his tiptoes, trying to see into the windows. He wondered if he should just stand there and wait or if he should go up onto that little platform step and knock on the narrow metal door. He sure was busting to get inside and check things out.

"Wait here," he said to Boo.

He climbed onto the step and knocked on the door.

Walter's face appeared in the window. "Elvis!" he hollered. "That skinny-headed ding-dong kid is here."

"Walter Jewell!" a woman yelled from somewhere inside. "If you're needin' some soap in your mouth, you say that again."

The door of the motor home opened.

"I got to get my shoes on," Elvis said.

Popeye tried to peer around him and see inside. Then, as if the good Lord had sent an angel to

43

answer his prayers, Elvis's mother snapped, "For heaven's sake, Elvis, invite the boy in."

Elvis stepped aside, and Popeye climbed up into the Holiday Rambler and found himself in a world of wonder. All around him were kids and shoes and pillows and towels and cereal boxes and paper cups and dirty dishes and piles of clothes and magazines and board games. On one side of the motor home a bed was folded down out of the wall and heaped with blankets and scattered with playing cards and potato chip bags. On the other side was a table with booth-style seats, like in a diner. Giant plastic soda bottles and paper plates with half-eaten hot dogs and puddles of ketchup littered the table.

Beside the booth was a tiny television, strapped to the wall with a bungee cord. Behind it was a tiny stove and a tiny sink and a tiny refrigerator. Popeye felt like he was inside a dollhouse. He didn't say a single word, but in his head, he was saying, "This is awesome, and Elvis, you are so lucky. Trade places with me. Go live in my house with the heart-shaped water stain on the ceiling and Dooley on the couch and I will live here in this silver dollhouse."

Then he was snapped out of his daydream by Elvis's mother, who said, "I'm Glory Jewell."

She was sitting in a blue plaid chair up front next to the driver's seat, her feet propped on the folded-down bed and her hands resting on her stomach. She was a great big overstuffed pillow of a woman, the exact opposite of Velma, who was as hard and dried up as a peach pit. On the ceiling above her, a tiny fan whirred and rotated back and forth, blowing her thin dark curls off her forehead.

"You can call me Glory," she said, fanning herself with a magazine. "I bet you hadn't counted on get-tin' new neighbors, huh?" She grinned at Popeye.

"No, ma'am."

"Furman's supposedly coming up with a plan to get this thing out of the mud, but I got my doubts." She dabbed her neck with a paper towel. "I swear, if that husband of mine had an idea, it would die of loneliness."

Popeye wasn't sure if he should smile at that or not, so he did a little half-smile thing and shrugged his shoulders. Behind him, Walter and Willis were kicking each other on the bed, their legs flailing and their bare feet slapping each other's arms. Prissy was trying to grab something away from Shorty, and Calvin was standing on top of the kitchen counter writing on the ceiling with a marker.

"Calvin!" Glory snapped. "You got your stupid head on today?"

So Calvin jumped down onto the bed and landed on top of Willis and everybody was suddenly kicking and hollering and Elvis said, "Come on," to Popeye and flung the door open and disappeared outside.

Popeye followed him, stepping down out of that noisy silver dollhouse and out into the real world.

8

POPEYE AND ELVIS spent all morning at the creek. The first thing they did was dig under the pile of leaves to see if the little Yoo-hoo boat was still there.

It was.

Then they decided to build a bigger dam than the one they had built the day before. That way, if any other boats came down the creek, they would get trapped.

They piled up rocks and branches and mud until they had a real good dam.

"There," Elvis said. "That oughta do it."

The next thing they did was sit on the mossy

bank beside the creek and wait, while Boo curled up in the soft green ferns beside them and napped.

"How long you think we'll have to wait?" Popeye said.

Elvis tossed pebbles into the creek.

Plunk.

Plunk.

"Beats me," he said. "How long we been here?"

Popeye glanced up at the sky. "Beats me."

They sat and they waited and they sat and they waited and after a while, Elvis said, "Aw, heck, this is stupid. Let's go see where this creek comes from."

So the two boys and Boo made their way along the edge of the creek, farther and farther into the woods. Sometimes they had to push through pricker bushes or climb over fallen trees. Sometimes the creek went straight, and sometimes it curved around a corner and then straightened out again.

As he walked, Popeye could feel Velma's eyes on him, sharp as tacks. The farther he got into the woods, the sharper those tacks got. After a while, he could hear her voice, cutting through him like a knife.

Don't you be going too far into them woods, you hear?

48

There's snakes and I don't know what else back there.

But Popeye kept going.

The three of them walked and walked and walked, following the creek.

Elvis and Popeye and Boo.

One behind the other.

Finally, after it seemed like they'd walked about a million miles, Elvis said, "Dang! Let's stop."

Popeye tried not to look too relieved when he said, "Okay."

"Let's mark this spot so we'll know how far we came," Elvis said.

They found two big branches and placed them beside the creek, one crossed over the other, to make an X. Then they turned around and headed back down the creek.

Elvis walked in that heavy-footed, head-hanging way of his, not talking. Popeye hummed a little as he walked. Just a hum, hum, hum, no-name tune. Every once in a while, Boo stopped to drink from the creek, making big slurping noises.

They hadn't gone very far when Popeye noticed something out of the corner of his eye.

Something yellow and brown and blue.

A boat!

A Yoo-hoo boat!

"There's a boat!" he hollered, making Elvis jump. "Look! Over yonder! A boat!"

Elvis stepped down into the water, shoes and all, and scooped it up. Then he climbed back onto the creek bank and he and Popeye examined it.

The boat was perfectly made, just like the first one. And tucked inside was a tiny square of paper, just like before.

Popeye could hardly keep still as he watched Elvis unfold the paper.

Once.

Twice.

Three times.

There was the same sloppy handwriting.

The same blue colored pencil.

The boys read out loud together:

"Princess . . . Queen . . . T-Bone"

9

"Y'ALL ARE IN TROUBLE."

"Y'all are in trouble."

Prissy and Calvin and Walter and Willis and Shorty danced around Popeye and Elvis, their faces beaming with delight.

Popeye's stomach clumped up into a knot, and worry fluttered around him like a moth around a flame.

Elvis, on the other hand, looked like worry was meant for anybody else but him. He waved off those kids with an annoyed flap of his hand, like swatting at gnats.

Prissy skipped after them as they made their way up the side of the gravel road.

"Your grandmamma was gonna call the police," Prissy said to Popeye, pronouncing the word *PO-leese*, loud and dramatic.

"Yeah, and she was banging on our door and hollering in our windows," Walter said.

"What was she saying?" Popeye said. His voice came out quiet and whiny and worried.

All the kids took turns hollering like Velma.

"You in there, Popeye?"

"Get out here right now, Popeye."

"I'm gonna skin you alive, Popeye."

"You got till the count of three, Popeye."

"So what?" Elvis said.

So what?

Why hadn't Popeye thought of saying that? It was the perfect I'm-not-one-bit-worried kind of thing to say.

So he said it, too.

"So what?"

Only, when he said it, it didn't sound nearly as not-worried as when Elvis said it.

"And Mama is mad as a hornet at you, Elvis."

Prissy galloped in circles around them. "You were supposed to help Daddy fix that tire jack."

Elvis shoved her aside. "So what?" he said.

"Yeah, so what?" Popeye said.

"Where y'all been, anyways?" Calvin said.

Elvis stopped and glared into Calvin's face. "Nowhere."

"Yeah," Popeye said. "Nowhere."

Elvis pushed his way through all the kids, and Popeye followed him. When they got to the motor home, Elvis climbed up the ladder on the back and sat cross-legged on the roof. Popeye stayed below, trying hard to push his worry away and look like somebody who says "So what?" and means it. But he was pretty sure it wasn't working. He was pretty sure he looked like someone scared to go home and face the wrath of Velma.

wrath: *noun*; extreme anger

That had been one of Velma's words a few weeks ago.

Popeye had learned it, and now he was going to go home to face it.

53

***

Velma's wrath had been swift and mighty.

She had met him at the door with arms crossed and foot tapping, her lips squeezed together into a hard line.

Popeye's feet had felt like cinder blocks as he made his way up the front steps and into the house.

The clock ticked.

A couple of flies buzzed around a half-eaten sandwich on the coffee table.

Boo flopped down on his bed by the woodstove with a grunt.

And then Velma let her wrath fly.

". . . been calling you and calling you . . ."

". . . told you not to go . . ."

". . . that hooligan hippie boy . . ."

". . . got my hands full with Dooley and now you go and . . ."

Popeye sat on the couch, staring down at the dirt on his knees and letting the wrath swirl around him.

Finally, it stopped.

The clock ticked.

Boo snored.

Velma dropped into her easy chair and turned on the television.

Popeye went out on the porch and sat on the top step. Velma's wrath still hovered in the air like a swarm of hornets.

Popeye let out a big heaving sigh and propped his chin in his hands. He and Elvis had made plans to go back to the creek later that day.

Elvis could waltz out of the Holiday Rambler and trot on back to the creek without a care in the world.

But not him.

He was stuck here under a swarm of hornets, listening to the clock.

Tick.

Tick.

Tick.

10

ONE OF THE BEST THINGS about having Dooley
for an uncle was that he was very good at diverting
the wrath of Velma.

divert: *verb*; to cause to change course or turn
from one direction to another

Not five minutes after Popeye had gone out on
the porch and Velma had dropped into her easy
chair, the phone rang.

It was someone named Sergeant Greeley from
over at the Anderson County Sheriff's Department.

56

Popeye knew this because here is what he heard from his spot on the porch:

"Sergeant who?"

"Greeley?"

"I don't know any Sergeant Greeley."

"Sheriff's department?"

"What sheriff's department?"

"Anderson County?"

"Well, what in blazes . . . ?"

Then Velma's voice went from grouchily irritated to whopping mad.

"I wish to sweet heaven above I *didn't* know Dooley Odom," she yelled into the phone.

After a few more lines like "Oh, for criminy's sake" and "I need this like I need a hole in the head," Velma slammed a few doors and muttered some nasty things about Dooley and came out on the porch with her purse and car keys.

When she told Popeye to stay in the house while she was gone, he didn't say "yes, ma'am."

He didn't nod.

He didn't move a muscle.

But in his head, his thoughts danced.

Anderson County?

Thirty minutes to get there.

Thirty minutes to get back.

One hour.

He had one whole hour to waltz out of the house and trot on back to the creek without a care in the world.

Like Elvis.

Popeye sent a silent message of thanks to Dooley as he watched Velma go roaring out of the driveway and up the road, dirt and gravel flying.

✳ ✳ ✳

"Calvin and them are gonna try and follow us," Elvis said. "I just know it." He glanced over his shoulder.

"Maybe we shouldn't go back there now," Popeye said.

"We got to." Elvis pushed through the tall weeds and jumped over a log.

"We could go tomorrow," Popeye said.

"No way." Elvis turned to face Popeye. "Look," he said. "If you don't want to come, that's fine by me. Go on home. But my dad is gonna get that motor home out of the mud any time now and I want to find out where them boats came from."

Popeye looked down at the ground. Why did he have to be such a baby about stuff? he wondered. Why was he so scared of Velma and her wrath? What had happened to all that waltzing and trotting he had planned on doing not ten minutes ago?

Why couldn't he be more like Elvis?

They followed the fern-lined path into the woods. The air felt cool and damp. Popeye breathed in the earthy smell of it.

As soon as they got within sight of the creek, Popeye could see the boat, floating there in the little pond created by the dam.

"Hot dang!" Elvis raced toward the creek. "Another boat!" he hollered.

Popeye ran after him, the flutter of worry in his stomach turning to a flutter of joy and excitement. When they got to the creek, Popeye darted in front of Elvis and leaped into the water, shoes and all.

Elvis looked a little annoyed, but Popeye grinned at him as he stood in the creek with minnows dart-

ing around his ankles and held the boat up proudly
in the palm of his hand.

"Is there a note?" Elvis said.

Popeye peered into the boat. "Yep."

He climbed out of the creek, set the boat down on
the mossy bank, and unfolded the note.

Once.

Twice.

Three times.

The boys read the note out loud together:

"Float like a butterfly.
Sting like a bee."

11

qualm: *noun*; an uneasy feeling of doubt, worry, or fear, especially about one's own conduct

Popeye had been having a lot of qualms lately.

Yesterday, he had qualms about going so far into the woods where he wasn't supposed to go.

Then he had qualms about leaving the house when Velma told him not to.

And he had qualms about looking for whoever was sending those little Yoo-hoo boats like Elvis wanted to.

So many qualms.

Popeye's stomach didn't feel too good.

He finished his milk and went into the living room to lie to Velma.

Another qualm.

"Can I go over to the ball field behind the school?" he said, keeping his eyes on the faded green rug.

Velma put down her crossword puzzle and looked over the top of her glasses at Popeye. "What for?" she said.

Popeye shrugged.

Velma narrowed her eyes. "With who?"

Popeye glanced at Velma's stack of crossword puzzle magazines.

He glanced at the lady on television mopping her floor and singing about how much fun it was.

He glanced at Dooley's muddy work boots under the coffee table.

"Just me," he said.

Velma was going to say no.

Ever since she had brought Dooley home from the sheriff's department yesterday, she'd been flinging her wrath around the house like crazy. Dooley, of course, was staying out back in his trailer so none of that wrath would come his way. (Where it right-fully belonged, in Popeye's opinion.)

Velma breathed in real deep and let out a big sigh. "Popeye," she said. "I am a beat-down woman. My spirit is broken. My patience is worn thin. I am done."

Popeye felt a little ray of hope starting to shine in that house of wrath.

He kept quiet and waited.

"Go," Velma said. "Just go." She dropped her head onto the back of the chair and closed her eyes.

Popeye felt a whoop trying to work its way out of him, but he clamped his mouth shut. Then he motioned for Boo to come with him and raced off to the Holiday Rambler.

Elvis sat by the side of the road, looking glum. His father, Furman Jewell, sat beside him, wiping the sweat off the back of his neck with a dirty red bandanna. Tools were spread out in the weeds around them. A crowbar. A shovel. A pickax. A car jack.

"Hey," Popeye called.

Elvis looked up. "Hey," he said. "I can't go. I've got to help my dad."

Furman Jewell waved his hand at Elvis. "Ah, go on." He looked over at the still-tilted, still-stuck-in-the-mud motor home and shook his head. "I've got to come up with Plan B."

Elvis jumped up and took off toward the creek. "Come on," he called over his shoulder.

* * *

Except for a few rotting leaves and a school of silvery minnows, the little pool formed by the dam in the creek was empty.

No boat.

The boys stood on the bank of the creek and stared down into the clear water. Boo stood beside them, snapping at the gnats circling around his face.

"Maybe whoever sent the boats is gone now," Popeye said.

Elvis shook his head. "Naw, I bet you anything we find another boat today."

"Maybe whoever sent the boats is tired of making 'em."

"No way," Elvis said.

"Or maybe they got tired of drinking Yoo-hoo."

Elvis kicked some dirt into the creek, making the

minnows dart around. "Look," he said, "if you don't want to go with me, then go on home. Play with Prissy if you want to."

"I didn't say I didn't want to go." Popeye tried to sound tough, like Elvis, but he just sounded squeaky.

"Then come on." Elvis pushed through the bushes and started off up the side of the creek.

Before long, they came to the spot where they had left the two branches crossed to form an X.

They kept going.

After a while, the weeds and bushes and trees began to get thicker, making it harder to follow the creek. Every so often, they had to mash down some pricker bushes or snap off branches so Boo could get through.

"I should've brought my hatchet," Elvis said.

Hatchet?

Elvis had a hatchet?

Popeye wished Velma would let him have stuff like that.

The thought of Velma stirred up all those qualms of his, making him feel not-so-good again. Just as he was thinking maybe he should tell Elvis he was sick and go on back home, Elvis let out a whoop.

"A boat!" he hollered, stepping down into the creek and scooping up the Yoo-hoo boat.

Popeye's stirred-up qualms settled down, and he waited for Elvis to bring the boat over and unfold the note.

Just like before.

Once.

Twice.

Three times.

And just like before, they read the note together:

"Indians smoke pipes."

12

"THAT DON'T MAKE one lick of sense," Elvis said, stuffing the note into his pocket.

Popeye examined the boat.

Perfect.

Just like the others.

That did it. He was ready to push all his qualms aside and find out who was sending the perfect Yoo-hoo boats down the creek. He felt a burst of courage lifting him up and pushing him forward.

"Let's go," he said, hurrying on up the side of the creek with Boo trotting along behind him.

The noonday sun was high overhead, sending

streams of light through the trees and dancing along the tops of the ferns that lined the winding creek.

"Shoot," Elvis said. "This creek's liable to go all the way to China."

Popeye squinted up the creek. It went on and on.

More water.

More rocks.

More trees.

More ferns.

His burst of courage had begun to fizzle out. It grew dimmer and dimmer until it was gone and all his qualms came flooding back.

"Yeah," he said. "China."

Elvis hurled a stick into the creek. "Dadgum it," he said. "Soon as my dad gets our motor home out of the mud, we're leaving. I sure do want to know who this boatbuilding cuckoo bird is."

Popeye hurled a stick into the creek, too. "Do you think it's a kid?" he said.

Elvis shrugged. "Probably."

"A boy or a girl?"

"Boy."

Popeye studied the Yoo-hoo boat, trying to imagine the cuckoo bird who had made it.

"I'm tired and hungry," Elvis said. "Let's mark this spot and go on back."

* * *

"Where y'all been?" Prissy came running toward them, her tap shoes clacking on the gravel.

"To China," Elvis said.

"Fibber." Prissy skipped along behind them. When they got to the motor home, the other kids ran over, stirring up dust and elbowing each other to get to Boo.

"Your grandma is gonna make your no-good uncle help Daddy get the Holiday Rambler out of the mud," Calvin said.

Popeye felt an unexpected wave of anger flood over him. "Don't call my uncle no-good," he said.

"Your grandma did," Calvin said.

"Yeah," Walter said, "and she called him a criminal, too."

"And a lazy bum moocher," Willis said.

"She said he's about as useful as a steering wheel on a mule." Calvin nudged Willis. "Ain't that right, Willis?"

Willis nodded.

"Yeah," Shorty said, grabbing Boo's tail and swinging it around and around like a jump rope. Boo gave him a dirty look, but he didn't move.

"Your grandma's had it up to *here* with your uncle Dooley." Prissy sliced her hand over her head full of springy curls. "She said he's got to get all his friends to come over and get us out of the mud."

Elvis turned to Popeye. "That means we've got to finish what we were doing," he said.

"What *were* y'all doing?" Calvin smacked Shorty on the arm to make him quit swinging Boo's tail.

"It's a secret," Elvis said.

"You can't keep secrets," Prissy said.

"Says who?" Elvis narrowed his eyes and stuck his face down close to hers.

She jabbed her fists into her waist and glared back at him. "That's the *rules*," she said.

Elvis thumped her on the side of the head and said, "They don't call me the Royal Rule Breaker for nothing, right, Popeye?"

Popeye nodded. "Right."

Royal Rule Breaker.

He'd give anything to be a Royal Rule Breaker.

"Let's go get some lunch," Elvis said.

* * *

Popeye sat on the bench in the diner booth of the Holiday Rambler and ate a jelly sandwich. The other kids used their old paper plates with their names written on them in crayon, but Popeye ate right off the sticky table.

Glory sat in her big plaid chair up front and wrote in a spiral notebook. "What rhymes with *car*?" she said.

"Far," Prissy said, arranging potato chips in a neat circle around the edge of her plate.

"Bar," Shorty hollered from under the bed, where he had made a little cave lined with blankets. He tossed the crusts from his bread out to Boo, who gobbled them up.

"Jar," Willis said.

"That's stupid," Calvin said. "What's she gonna say about a jar?"

Glory was writing a country-western song.

She'd write a little and then sing a little.

Write a little, then sing a little.

Popeye thought writing country-western songs might be another way for Velma to keep from cracking up. He was going to suggest it once her wrath settled down.

"Popeye and Elvis are keeping a secret," Prissy said, mashing her potato chips into crumbs with her thumb.

"That's their right as American citizens," Glory said. "What rhymes with *heaven*?"

"Kevin?" Popeye said.

Glory jabbed her pen at him. "Kevin!" she said. "That's perfect! This two-timing truck driver can be named Kevin." She scribbled something in her notebook. "Thank you, Popeye."

Popeye beamed.

He hadn't beamed in a long time.

And then he had a sudden flash of longing. Of wanting more than anything to travel the world in this silver dollhouse with Glory and the gang, writing country-western songs and playing cards and breaking rules instead of waking up every day in Fayette, South Carolina.

But, of course, that was never going to happen.

So for now, he might as well enjoy having a small adventure with Elvis.

Now, more than ever, Popeye was determined to find whoever was sending those perfect little Yoo-hoo boats down the creek.

13

avuncular: *adjective*; of or relating to an uncle

Popeye figured that Velma had probably chosen that vocabulary word because she knew it would come in handy someday.

It did.

The avuncular atmosphere in the house was not too good.

Dooley sat on the couch staring at the blank television screen while Velma ranted, her bony arms flailing.

". . . high time you got your act together . . ."

". . . make yourself useful for once in your life . . ."

". . . next time, don't call me . . ."

She went on and on about how he'd better round up some of his bum friends and help the Jewells get their motor home out of the mud. Then she ended with a big, loud "had it up to here," slicing her hand over her head exactly the way Prissy had demonstrated earlier that day.

Popeye stayed in the kitchen, peeking into the living room every few minutes. He couldn't decide whether or not to check in with Velma before going back in the woods with Elvis. If he did, he might have to lie, which didn't seem like a good idea.

All things considered, he decided to just go on back outside.

Elvis was waiting by the shed with Boo.

"What'd she say?" He pulled a tick off Boo and flicked it into the weeds.

"She's still yelling at Dooley."

"Then let's go."

The two boys headed up the path toward the woods with Boo strolling along behind them. When they got to the creek, they both let out a whoop.

A yellow, brown, and blue Yoo-hoo boat floated in the creek. The water had begun to spill around the edges of the dam and trickle on down into the creek bed below it, but the boat sat safely wedged among the rocks.

Elvis scooped it up and opened the note.

The boys read:

"7 7 7 7 7 7 7"

Elvis stamped his foot. "Now I'm getting mad," he said. "This ain't nothing but a bunch of jibberty-jibe."

But Popeye wasn't so sure. Why would someone send jibberty-jibe down the creek in perfect little Yoo-hoo boats? The notes must mean *something*.

"Maybe the number seven is a clue," he said. "Like, go seven feet to the seventh tree and pass seven bushes or something like that."

"Or maybe, walk seven miles for seven hours seven days a week for nothing," Elvis said, tucking the note back inside the boat.

"Let's try one more time," Popeye said.

So they scooped up the pile of leaves where the other boats were and added this one. They carefully covered them again, then started off up the side of the creek.

Before they had gotten to the first spot they had marked with an X, they found another boat.

4 and 20 blackbirds

Elvis picked up a small branch from the side of the creek and snapped it in half by cracking it over his knee. Then he hurled both pieces into the woods.

Hard.

"I can't figure these dang notes out," he said. "Not one of 'em means *nothing*."

Popeye read the note again.

It must mean *something*.

But what?

He refolded the note and put it back inside the boat. "Maybe we should look for some blackbirds," he said, glancing up into the trees.

Elvis shook his head and stomped off up the side of the creek, kicking at rocks and branches and leaves and muttering stuff under his breath.

Popeye flattened the boat and tucked it into the pocket of his shirt. "Come on, Boo," he said, running to catch up with Elvis.

They walked in silence. Popeye kept a close eye on the creek, searching among the rocks and tree roots for another Yoo-hoo boat.

"There's one!" he hollered, lying on his stomach and reaching down into the water to scoop up the boat. He unfolded the note and read it out loud:

"Dead dogs live here."

Dead dogs?

Popeye and Elvis looked at each other, wide-eyed.

"That does it," Elvis said. "I ain't going back until we find out who's sending these boats."

Popeye read the note again, "Dead dogs live here."

This was the best note yet.

He flattened the boat, tucked it into his pocket with the other one, and followed Elvis up the side of the creek.

They hadn't gone far when Elvis stopped and pointed. "A path!" he hollered.

A narrow path led from the creek through a tangle of scrub pines and pricker bushes. They had walked right by this spot last time, not even noticing the path.

"Let's see where it goes," Elvis said.

"I don't know," Popeye said. "There might be poison oak and snakes and stuff in there." He could feel Velma hovering in the air around him, pointing out the dangers that lurked under every leaf and rock.

Then, just as he was worrying about how to turn around and go home without looking like a baby, he spotted something along the edge of the path.

Indian pipes!

Clusters of little white plants that looked like smoking pipes popped up out of the rich, moist soil along both sides of the path.

"Look!" Popeye said. "Those are called Indian pipes."

Elvis squinted at the plants. "So?"

"Indians smoke pipes!" Popeye grinned at Elvis. "That note was a clue about this path."

The boys let out a whoop and high-fived each other.

"Come on!" Elvis hollered as he trotted up the path and disappeared into the woods.

Popeye raced off after Elvis with Boo trotting along behind.

14

POPEYE AND ELVIS made their way along the narrow path that snaked its way through the woods. Clusters of the little white Indian pipes were scattered among the ferns and moss. Before long, the path grew wider and rocks neatly lined the edges on both sides.

Suddenly, both boys stopped.

Nailed to a tree in front of them was a sign.

KEEP OUT

Painted in red with big crooked letters.

Boo sat beside Popeye, his tail brushing back and forth in the dirt.

"We better not go any farther," Popeye said.

"Are you crazy?" Elvis said. "We've come all this way. We can't stop now."

Popeye looked down at Boo.

Boo yawned.

Popeye shrugged. "Come on, Boo," he said.

They continued on up the rock-lined path until it curved around a cluster of rhododendrons and ended.

Elvis stopped.

Popeye stopped.

Boo stopped.

They were in the backyard of the craziest-looking house Popeye had ever seen. The middle of it looked like a regular house. Small. Square. White. The bottom half was stained orange from the red-dirt yard around it.

But sticking out from every side of the regular-looking house were crooked little rooms pieced together with old lumber, sheets of plywood, jagged-edged scraps of tar paper, and a metal stop sign riddled with bullet holes.

diverse: *adjective*; showing a great deal of variety

That house was definitely diverse.

"Let's check it out," Elvis said.

Popeye followed Elvis into the yard of the crazy-looking house with his heart thumping.

Maybe he should turn around and go home right now.

Maybe he should just go sit in Velma's easy chair and listen to the clock ticking away the minutes.

Maybe he just wasn't cut out for small adventures.

But he forced his feet to keep moving.

Blue floral sheets flapped in the breeze on a clothesline.

Four scrawny chickens pecked at pebbles in the dirt beside a kudzu-covered shed.

Big noisy blackbirds perched on a flimsy chicken-wire fence surrounding a small vegetable garden.

And a diverse collection of junk was scattered all around the yard:

A wheelbarrow filled with dirty rainwater.

A bicycle with a bent wheel.

A rusty saw.

An aluminum lawn chair with the seat missing.

A garden hose in a tangled heap.

A bent-up beach umbrella.

"Let's go around front," Elvis said.

Don't go, Popeye. Don't go, Popeye.

That's what Popeye heard inside his head.

But his feet kept moving, following Elvis up the gravel driveway that ran along the side of the house, past a dented brown station wagon, and around the corner of the house to the front yard.

Then Elvis stopped.

And Popeye stopped.

And Boo stopped.

Kneeling in the yard, scooping dirt into a jar, was a little girl with wings.

15

THE GIRL LOOKED UP and met the boys' wide-eyed stares with an uninterested blink, then went back to her dirt scooping.

"Hey," Elvis said.

"Hey," she said, not looking up.

Her gravelly voice didn't match her delicate look: small and thin, like a twig.

She wore a grimy canvas hat pulled down over her ears.

And wings.

Gauzy yellow butterfly wings, tattered and dirty, dotted here and there with clusters of shiny gold sequins and attached to the girl by straps that slipped over her arms like those of a backpack.

"What you doing?" Elvis said.

She stopped scooping and looked up at Elvis from where she knelt on the ground. "Scooping dirt into a jar," she said.

"How come?"

"Because I like to." She scooped one last handful of dirt into the jar, ran her palm over the top to level the dirt, and screwed the lid on. Then she stood up and wiped her dirty hands on her shorts. Scraggly wisps of red hair clung to her neck beneath the hat.

"Why do you have them wings on?" Elvis said.

She looked over her shoulder at the wings, as if she had forgotten they were there. Then she picked up the jar of dirt, walked past the boys, and disappeared around the corner of the house.

Elvis frowned and shook his head. "She's crazy," he said.

But there was something about the girl with wings that took the qualms out of Popeye and replaced them with an unusually adventurous spirit.

"Come on," he said, motioning for Elvis to follow him.

When they got to the backyard, the girl was drinking from the hose, the water splattering mud onto her skinny legs. When she finished drinking, she took the jar of dirt over to the porch. The butterfly wings flapped slightly as she walked. She placed the jar on the edge of the back porch, carefully lining it up next to three other jars of dirt.

"Y'all want a Yoo-hoo?" the girl said.

Popeye's adventurous spirit did a cartwheel. He grinned at Elvis. "She's the one who made the boats," he whispered.

Elvis nodded solemnly. Then he turned to the girl and said, "Sure."

"Wait right here." She opened the squeaky screen door and disappeared inside the crazy-looking house.

Elvis didn't hesitate. He leaped up the steps two at a time and waited outside the door.

Normally, Popeye would have hesitated.

But today wasn't normal.

Today, he leaped up the steps two at a time. But before he got to the top, the girl poked her head out

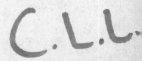

of the door and said, "That dog can't come on the porch. He looks like my uncle Haywood."

Popeye looked down at Boo, who sat forlornly at the bottom of the steps, gazing up at him with those watery, sad-dog eyes of his. "Sorry, fella," he said. Then he went up on the porch to drink a Yoo-hoo.

16

THE THREE OF THEM sat on the top step of the porch. Music from a radio drifted through the screen door from inside the house.

The girl poked Popeye in the arm with a skinny elbow and said, "What's your name?"

"Popeye."

"That's dumb."

Elvis spewed Yoo-hoo into the air and slapped his knee, laughing.

"What's *your* name?" the girl said to Elvis.

When he told her, she said, "That's dumber." She tilted her head back and gulped down the last of her Yoo-hoo drink. "*I* am Princess Starletta Rainey."

"Well, what do you know, Popeye?" Elvis said. "Here we are, sittin' on the porch with a princess."

"I am *called* Starletta," the girl said. She flapped both palms out in front of Popeye and Elvis and said, "Give me those."

The boys finished their drinks and placed the empty cartons into Starletta's hands.

"Did you make them boats in the creek?" Elvis said.

Starletta hopped down the porch steps. "Yep."

"Show us how to make 'em."

"No." Starletta reached up under the porch and pulled out a plastic milk crate filled with empty Yoo-hoo cartons. She tossed the three cartons into the crate and said, "Want me to show you how to make a boat?"

Elvis looked at Popeye, twirled a finger around his ear, and whispered, "Cuckoo. Cuckoo."

Starletta held up one finger. "First," she said, "you drink the Yoo-hoo."

Elvis poked Popeye with his elbow again and said, "Duh."

Starletta shot him a glare.

"Next," she said, holding up two fingers, "you unfold the top to be the front of the boat." She demonstrated.

"Then . . ." She held up three fingers. "You cut out part of the side, like this." She took a pair of rusty scissors out of the crate and cut off part of the Yoo-hoo carton.

"There!" She held the little boat out in the palm of her hand.

Elvis said, "Cool!" and Popeye said, "Wow!"

Then the three of them sat on the porch steps and made Yoo-hoo boats.

Elvis kept asking Starletta about the notes she had put inside the boats. What did "float like a butterfly" mean? How come she wrote all those sevens? Where are the dead dogs?

But Starletta wouldn't answer. She just kept unfolding and cutting and humming like Popeye and Elvis weren't even there.

Popeye could tell that Elvis was irritated as all get-out. But it didn't bother him one little bit that Starletta wouldn't talk about the notes. He wanted to figure them out by himself.

He had already guessed the one about the Indian pipes.

And the very first one was just Starletta making a joke: *Yoo-hoo! Ha! Ha!*

Suddenly, Popeye snapped his fingers. "Float like a butterfly!" he said, pointing to Starletta's wings. " 'Cause you like butterflies, right?"

Starletta jumped off the steps and bounced around the yard on her toes, punching the air with her fists, the scruffy butterfly wings flapping in the breeze.

Elvis rolled his eyes and made that finger-circling cuckoo motion around his ear again.

But Popeye watched Starletta and thought of a vocabulary word.

mesmerize: *verb*; to hold the attention of someone to the exclusion of all else

Starletta bouncing around the yard in those butterfly wings mesmerized him.

She stopped suddenly, tilted her chin up, and recited into the air, "Float like a butterfly, sting like

a bee. Your hands can't hit what your eyes can't see."
She arched her eyebrows at Popeye and Elvis. "Get
it?" she said.

"No," Elvis snapped.

"Muhammad Ali," she said. "The greatest boxer
of all time." She punched the air again. "He made up
that poem."

"Boxers don't make up girl poems," Elvis said.

Starletta stomped off to the vegetable garden,
wings flapping. She took her hat off and began picking beans and dropping them into her hat. Then she
came back over to the porch and dumped the beans
into a metal bowl on the steps.

Popeye was thinking about the notes, trying to
remember each one. He'd figured out three of them.
How many were left?

Elvis must have been thinking the very same
thing at the very same time, because he tossed a Yoo-
hoo boat into the crate and said, "So where are the
dead dogs?"

"I *might* tell you," Starletta said. "And I *might* tell
him." She pointed at Popeye. "But I'm not telling
those kids."

"What kids?" Elvis narrowed his eyes at her.

"Those kids in the bushes over yonder."

Popeye looked over at the bushes just in time to see five curly-haired heads duck down out of sight.

Prissy, Calvin, Walter, Willis, and Shorty.

17

ELVIS RACED OVER to the bushes and started hollering and flailing and kicking and thumping everyone on the head.

Words were flying.

Sneaky

No-good

Slimy

Dirty

Stinking

Spies

Popeye and Starletta watched as the tangle of kids punched and kicked and tumbled in a heap around the yard, stirring up swirls of dust and sending the chickens squawking.

Starletta slapped her knee and let out a "Woo-hoo!"

Finally, Calvin hollered, "Truce!" and everyone stopped, panting and gasping and sniffling.

Elvis got in one last whack at Willis, and then Starletta said, "I guess y'all can't read."

Prissy and Calvin and Walter and Willis and Shorty stared at Starletta. She jammed her hat back on her head and jabbed her thumb toward the sign at the edge of the woods. "That says 'Keep Out.' "

Prissy skipped over to the back porch steps and peered inside the milk crate. "Let me make a Yoo-hoo boat," she said.

"No!" Elvis hollered, and the two of them started going at it again until Starletta yelled, "Uncle Haywood's in the garden!"

Elvis and Prissy stopped with their hands in midair, and everyone turned to look at the garden.

Boo was digging, his rear end up in the air and his front paws working fast and furious, sending up a spray of dirt and pebbles and pole bean vines.

Popeye raced over and grabbed Boo by the collar. "Dang, Boo," he said.

He dragged his dog out of the garden and said, "Sorry," but Starletta seemed to have forgotten all about Boo. She was gathering rocks from the yard and tucking them into her pockets.

"What are you gonna do with those rocks?" Calvin said.

"Throw 'em at you, probably," Prissy said, grinning over at Starletta. "Right?" she added.

"Is he a blackbird?" Starletta said.

"No, he's a dodo bird," Walter said.

Calvin punched him, and there was another brief whirlwind of dust as the boys wrestled.

"When those nasty blackbirds come squawking around our garden again, my daddy's gonna bake them in a pie," Starletta said.

"A pie?" Prissy picked up a rock and handed it to Starletta.

"A blackbird pie." Starletta hurled a rock up in the air. It landed on the rusty tin roof of the house with a loud *thwang*. "Four and twenty blackbirds baked in a pie," she sang.

The Yoo-hoo note!

Popeye looked over at Elvis, but he was kicking at the dirt and glaring at his brothers.

"Who wants to see my lucky walls?" Starletta said.

"I do!" Prissy called.

"I do!" Calvin hollered.

Walter and Willis and Shorty waved their hands and hopped around, and they all clamored up the back steps after Starletta, who had already disappeared inside.

"Come on," Elvis said, running after them.

Popeye wasn't about to be the only one who didn't go inside, but it took all his strength to shut out the voice of Velma, yelling inside his head: *Don't you never ever go following any strangers anywhere. You hear me?*

But he managed to do it.

Shut the door on Velma's words.

Slam!

Then he bounded up the steps, leaving Boo sitting forlornly in the yard.

* * *

Popeye stepped through Starletta's back door and could not get his eyes to look fast enough at all the stuff inside her kitchen. Every inch of counter and table and floor had something just begging to be looked at.

Prissy and the boys went crazy, running around picking things up and checking things out. Even Elvis quit his scowling and gazed around him in awe and admiration.

A giant pink teddy bear.

A rusty tricycle.

Plastic sunflowers.

A chipped, concrete flamingo.

An inflatable Santa Claus.

Golf clubs.

A birdhouse.

A cowboy hat.

A wagon filled with flashlights.

plethora: *noun;* an excess of something

Starletta's kitchen was filled with a plethora of *stuff*.

All the others were so busy checking out the plethora that they didn't notice the most amazing thing of all. The walls of the little kitchen were covered with about a million number sevens.

Big ones.

Little ones.

Medium ones.

Painted in red.

Painted in black.

Written with pen.

Written with pencil.

On nearly every inch of every wall.

"My lucky walls," Starletta said.

Popeye grinned.

Another Yoo-hoo note!

7777777

The number 7 written seven times.

Starletta grabbed a red marker out of a coffee can on the kitchen counter and wrote a tiny number 7 on the wall next to the stove. "My lucky number."

Once again, Popeye was mesmerized. Here was a twig of a girl with butterfly wings, writing sevens on the wall.

"Starletta!" someone hollered from a room next to the kitchen.

"What?" Starletta hollered back.

"What're you doing in there?"

"Nothing."

"Who's in there with you?"

"Nobody."

A woman appeared in the doorway.

A tired-looking woman in a bathrobe.

"Y'all get on out of here," she said, throwing her arms wide as if to sweep them all out of the house.

Everyone scrambled.

Prissy jumped up off the floor, tossing a plastic snow globe back into a cardboard box. Calvin pushed Willis out of the way and jumped over stacks of magazines as he scrambled to the door. Walter yanked Shorty out from under the table, and Popeye and Elvis burst through the screen door with Starletta right behind them.

"So, who's that?" Elvis said when they all gathered in the yard. "The Queen?" He grinned at Popeye.

"Yes, she *is*," Starletta said. "Queen Starletta Rainey."

The kids giggled.

"And I reckon your dad's the king, right?" Elvis said.

Starletta unscrewed the lid from one of the jars on the porch and poured the dirt out into a little mound on the step. "No, he is *not*," she said. "He is T-Bone. Charlie the T-Bone Rainey. And he drives a chicken truck."

While the others were busy laughing about T-Bone and the chicken truck, Popeye was busy thinking about the note in the Yoo-hoo boat.

Princess . . . Queen . . . T-Bone

Starletta's family.

Princess, Queen, and T-Bone.

Now Popeye had figured out all of the notes but one.

The best one.

Dead dogs live here.

What in the world could that mean?

18

"SOMEBODY'S CALLING Y'ALL," Starletta said.

Sure enough, from somewhere out in the woods, someone was calling a name.

The someone was Velma.

The name was Popeye.

"Uh-oh," he said. "I got to go."

He raced toward the path at the edge of the yard, with Elvis, Prissy, Calvin, Walter, Willis, and Shorty right behind him.

Popeye's heart was pounding as he ran past the Indian pipes toward the creek. Boo galloped along beside him, ears flapping.

Velma's wrath-filled voice thundered through

the woods, trampling the ferns and crashing into trees.

When he got to the creek, Popeye stopped.

Boo stopped.

Elvis, Prissy, Calvin, Walter, Willis, and Shorty stopped.

"Listen, y'all," Popeye said. "Don't tell Velma about Starletta, okay?"

Elvis nodded solemnly. "Okay."

"Maybe," Calvin said.

Elvis punched him in the arm with a knuckle.

Then Popeye took a deep breath and walked around the curve in the path to meet his fate.

* * *

Velma had thumped Popeye in the head.

Thoink!

Like thumping a watermelon.

He'd looked down at his sneakers.

She'd thumped again.

Thoink!

Then she'd let fly with an avalanche of angry words. She'd been looking for him for hours. She'd been worried sick that he'd drowned in the creek.

He had no business hanging around all those wild kids. He'd better get himself on home in a hurry and stay there.

He had followed her back to the house, his head hanging, while Elvis and the others ran off to the Holiday Rambler.

And now here he was the next day, staring up at the heart-shaped stain on the ceiling of his bedroom.

"George V, Edward VIII, George VI . . ." drifted through the bedroom wall from the living room.

"Dead dogs live here," Popeye whispered.

Boo's ears perked up.

"Dead dogs live here," Popeye whispered again.

He got off the bed and looked out the window. The once-muddy yard had dried into hard slabs of red dirt. Patches of brown grass and weeds poked through here and there. Every now and then, a grasshopper sprang up and buzzed through the thick, still air before disappearing into the weeds again.

Popeye looked down the road in the direction of the Holiday Rambler. He wished he were in that silver motor home, playing cards with Elvis in the diner booth. Eating potato chips off a paper plate with his name written on it in crayon. Helping Glory Jewell write country-western songs.

But here he was in his bedroom, listening to Velma recite the kings and queens of England in chronological order.

Popeye flopped back down on the bed.

Pssst.

Popeye sat up. "What was that?" he said to Boo.

Boo ambled over to the window, tail wagging.

"*Pssst*, Popeye." Elvis's voice came through the open window from the bushes outside.

Popeye hurried over. "Hey," he whispered.

"Calvin and them rode their bikes to the Quiki Mart, so you and me can go on back to Starletta's without them following us."

"I got to stay in my room," Popeye said. "Velma's still mad."

"Yeah, but guess what?" Elvis said. "She told my dad he could count on Dooley to help him dig out the motor home. *And* . . ." He wiggled his eyebrows and grinned. "She said she's going to drive over to Simpsonville today to pick Dooley up at his friend's house and bring them both back to help." He jerked a thumb toward the road. "Soon as she leaves, come get me."

Popeye glanced over at his bedroom door.

He could feel it coming.

Another vocabulary word.

quandary: *noun*; a state of uncertainty over what to do in a difficult situation

He was about to find himself right smack in the middle of a quandary:

Should he go back to Starletta's with Elvis and find out about the dead dogs?

Or . . .

Should he stay here in his boring bedroom like Velma told him to?

19

WHEN THE BOYS got to Starletta's backyard, she was sleeping on a blanket, with chickens clucking around her and blackbirds flapping on the garden fence. She lay curled up on her side, her head resting on her hands and her butterfly wings flopping droopily behind her.

Ahem.

Elvis cleared his throat loudly.

Starletta opened her eyes.

Ahem.

Elvis cleared his throat again.

Starletta sat up, blinking in the morning sun.

Popeye and Elvis sat beside her. The blanket was hot and scratchy, with the faint scent of cedar.

"So," Popeye said, "where are the dead dogs?"

He leaned forward.

Waiting.

Waiting.

"Uh-oh!" Starletta snapped her fingers. Then she jumped up and ran around the side of the house.

Popeye and Elvis raced after her. When they got to the front yard, Starletta was marching in circles in a plastic swimming pool with Yoo-hoo boats swirling in the water around her. Beside the pool, a garden hose spewed water, flipping and slithering around the yard like a snake. Starletta's feet slapped the water, sending waterfalls over the sides of the pool, spilling into muddy puddles in the yard.

"I told you she was cuckoo," Elvis whispered.

But Popeye didn't think Starletta was cuckoo.

He thought she was eccentric.

eccentric: *adjective*; unconventional and slightly strange

"Where are the dead dogs?" he asked again.

Starletta swished the stick in the pool, splashing Popeye and Elvis. "In a dead dog place."

"Where's that?"

"Someplace."

"Someplace where?"

"Someplace."

"Show us."

"I only go there on Wednesdays," Starletta said.

Popeye's thoughts raced. What day was today? Was it Wednesday?

No.

It was Tuesday.

Dang!

"Today *is* Wednesday," Elvis said, winking at Popeye.

Starletta spun around and glared at him, her fists jammed into her waist. "You must think I'm stupid, little Elvis boy!" she hollered. "You think I don't know what day it is?"

Elvis shrugged.

"Will you show us tomorrow?" Popeye said.

Starletta poked the stick at the boats, making

them bob up and down like sailboats in the ocean. "Maybe."

"But I might be gone tomorrow," Elvis said. "Soon as Dooley and them dig our motor home out, we're leaving."

"What motor home?" Starletta said.

Elvis told her about the stuck-in-the-mud Holiday Rambler. But Starletta stayed firm.

"Only on Wednesdays," she said.

Popeye scrambled to think of some way to convince Starletta to show them the dead dog place on Tuesday instead of Wednesday.

But he couldn't.

All he could do was hope that the Holiday Rambler stayed in the mud for another day and that Dooley didn't have a miraculous change of character and turn into someone who could be counted on.

20

POPEYE AND ELVIS raced down the path that ran beside the creek. If Popeye didn't get back to the house before Velma got home, he was going to be a goner.

When they left the woods and made their way through the field toward the house, Popeye muttered "please, please, please" under his breath.

There was one thing he definitely did *not* want to see: Velma's car in the driveway.

There was one thing he definitely *did* want to see: the Holiday Rambler still stuck in the gravel road.

They raced around the shed in Popeye's backyard.

There was the driveway.

Velma's car was not there.

Popeye let out a whoop.

He and Elvis high-fived each other, gasping to catch their breath and grinning.

Then they ran down the road and around the corner.

There was the Holiday Rambler.

Tilted.

Stuck.

The boys high-fived each other again. Then Popeye dashed home to lie on his bed and stare at the ceiling until Velma got home.

✳ ✳ ✳

Dooley had not let Popeye down. He had not had a miraculous change of character. He had not turned into someone who could be counted on. He had, in fact, disappeared with his friend, Shifty. Velma had driven all over Simpsonville and all over Fayette and everywhere in between looking for them.

". . . don't know where I went wrong," Velma muttered under her breath as she cut the crusts off Popeye's cheese sandwich.

Popeye sat at the kitchen table and traced the ivy pattern on the vinyl place mat with his finger. Tomorrow was Wednesday. The day that Starletta went to the place where dead dogs live. How was he going to convince Velma to let him go back to the creek with Elvis tomorrow?

How?

How?

How?

Velma dropped the sandwich onto the paper towel in front of him.

"Um, Velma?" Popeye said.

Velma sank into the chair across from him and lifted her eyebrows.

"Um . . ." Popeye said again.

Velma lifted her eyebrows a little higher.

"Never mind." He took a bite of his sandwich.

Velma swatted at a fly that had landed on the sugar bowl. "That crazy family's been cooped up in that beehive trailer for five days," she said. "If I was that poor woman, I'd be in the loony bin by now."

She rolled up a crossword puzzle magazine and smacked it on the table. "Got him!" She scooped the fly into her hand and tossed it in the sink. Then she shuffled around the kitchen, putting away the bread and mayonnaise and muttering about all those wild kids and that poor woman who oughta be in the loony bin.

"But then, I reckon she must be needing groceries," Velma said.

Popeye felt a little flutter.

There was an itty-bitty crack in Velma's hard shell.

He had seen it happen before.

But his years of experience with Velma had taught him to keep quiet and leave her cracked shell alone. He tossed the last of his cheese sandwich under the table for Boo.

"You think she needs groceries?" Velma said.

Crack.

Popeye shrugged.

"Go on up there and ask her if she needs groceries."

Crack.

Popeye hurried to the back door. "But what if she *does* need groceries?" he said.

"Then I guess I'll have to give her a ride over to

Bi-Lo," Velma said. "Heaven forbid Dooley get his-self home and do something useful."

Bingo!

Velma's hard shell had cracked wide open.

Popeye jumped off the porch and trotted toward the road. "Come on, Boo."

"And Popeye . . ." Velma called from the back door.

Popeye stopped.

"If you see Dooley, tell him to start digging," she said.

"Yes, ma'am."

✳ ✳ ✳

When Popeye got to the Holiday Rambler, Calvin and Willis were up on the roof throwing acorns at Prissy, who darted gleefully from side to side in the road, her springy curls bouncing and her tap shoes clickety-clacking on the gravel.

"Missed me again," she hollered up at them.

"Hey, Popeye!" Calvin yelled down from the roof. "Catch!"

An acorn smacked Popeye in the arm, leaving a small red circle.

Popeye rubbed his arm. "I need to ask your mom

something," he said, climbing up on the step of the motor home and knocking on the narrow metal door.

"I told y'all to stay outside and I mean it," Glory Jewell yelled through the open window.

"It's me. Popeye."

The door opened. Elvis's hair stuck up every which way like he'd been sleeping. He yawned and scratched his stomach.

Popeye stepped inside. The motor home was hot and dark and smelled like something burnt. Furman Jewell sat in the diner booth, watching television. Walter and Shorty were sprawled on the fold-down bed, playing a card game that involved headlocks and knuckle noogies. Glory sat in her big plaid chair up front, fanning herself with her spiral notebook of country-western songs.

"Velma wants to know if you need groceries," Popeye said. "If you do, she'll drive you to Bi-Lo."

"That woman is a saint," Glory said.

* * *

As soon as Velma and Glory turned off the gravel road onto the highway, Popeye and Elvis raced behind the shed in Popeye's backyard to hide from Prissy and Calvin and the others.

Boo sat beside them, resting his big head in Popeye's lap, leaving a slobbery wet spot on his shorts.

"Okay, now listen," Elvis whispered. "We've got to get back to Starletta's tomorrow."

Popeye nodded.

Tomorrow was Wednesday.

Tomorrow would be their only chance to see the place where dead dogs live.

If they didn't go tomorrow, there wouldn't be another Wednesday for a whole week, and surely the Holiday Rambler would be long gone by then.

"We've got to figure out some way to get there without Calvin and them following us," Elvis said.

Popeye nodded. "Or Velma getting mad," he said.

connive: *verb*; to plot, scheme, or be in cahoots

He and Elvis were going to have to connive.

21

BEFORE POPEYE MET ELVIS, he had never been very good at conniving. But now here he was, sitting behind the shed, conniving up a storm.

"I have an idea," he said. "What if Boo gets lost in the woods?"

Boo's ears perked up.

"And so you and me have to go look for him."

"Okay!" Elvis said.

"But we can't lie," Popeye said. "Velma can smell a lie a mile away."

"Then how can we say Boo is lost in the woods if he ain't?"

Boo lifted his head at the sound of his name and blinked up at Elvis.

Popeye ran his hand over his prickly buzz cut, feeling his conniving skills getting better by the minute.

"We won't use the word *lost*. We'll just say Boo is back in the woods and we need to go find him."

"Okay!" Elvis said. "But what are we gonna do with Boo?"

Boo sat up and yawned.

"Well, I guess we'll have to put him back in the woods," Popeye said. "Then we won't be lying."

Boo cocked his head at Popeye.

Popeye looked away quickly before any qualms could come sneaking up on him and ruin everything.

* * *

That night, Velma was livid.

livid: *adjective*; furiously angry

Her livid voice burst right through the metal walls of Dooley's trailer and slithered across the darkness of the backyard and into the kitchen,

120

where Popeye stood at the counter spreading peanut butter onto graham crackers.

"Dooley better get out there first thing in the morning.

"His no-good criminal friend, Shifty, better be out there, too.

"They better get out there and help so those folks can leave."

Leave?

That word felt like a punch in the stomach.

Popeye had been so busy conniving about the dead dogs that he hadn't even thought about the motor home leaving.

Elvis leaving.

All those wild kids leaving.

He would walk around the curve in the road, and the Holiday Rambler with the shiny lightning bolts and the howling coyote would be gone. He would walk around the curve in the road, and there would only be weeds and gravel and a drainage ditch full of muddy water.

Popeye knelt down and took Boo's head in both hands. Boo looked at him with his soft, watery eyes and let out a big dog sigh.

Popeye explained to Boo again about what he and Elvis had connived. That they were going to take him into the woods, to a really nice spot by the creek. They were going to tie his leash to a tree (a really nice tree). Then they were going to leave him there, but only for a really, really, really short time.

Then Popeye was going to tell Velma that Boo was back in the woods.

Which would not be a lie.

And he was going to tell Velma that he and Elvis had to go get Boo, who was back in the woods.

Which would not be a lie.

Then, while everybody was busy trying to get the Holiday Rambler out of the mud, Popeye and Elvis would run back into the woods, get Boo (who would only have been sitting there for a really, really, really short time), and go on over to Starletta's.

Then Starletta would show them where the dead dogs live.

"I promise I won't leave you long," Popeye said.

Boo made a little snorting noise, and Popeye smiled. "You're a good dog, Boo." He patted Boo's head and scratched him behind the ears. "I sure do appreciate you helping me out."

Boo blinked.

"I'd do the same for you."

Blink.

"And I promise I'll do something real good for you."

Blink. Blink.

"Like cook you up some chicken livers or something."

The back door burst open, and the warm night air whooshed in. Velma stomped across the kitchen floor and yanked the refrigerator door open. She rummaged around inside it, moving pickle jars and soda cans, muttering about Dooley eating all the leftover spaghetti.

"Velma?" Popeye said.

"What?"

"Do we have any chicken livers?"

22

BY THE TIME Popeye got to the Holiday Rambler the next morning, everyone was gathered around watching Dooley and Shifty and Furman digging and grunting and wiping sweat off their foreheads. Boards and crowbars and car jacks lay scattered in the weeds by the side of the road.

Prissy, Calvin, Walter, Willis, and Shorty chased each other and jumped over the ditch and fiddled with the car jacks while Glory sat in a lawn chair and hollered at them.

Velma stood beside the motor home with her fists jammed into her waist, just daring Dooley to quit digging.

Elvis trotted over to Popeye. "Listen," he whispered. "We've got to be real careful that Calvin and them don't see us leave or they'll follow us for sure."

"Okay."

"Is Boo back in the woods?"

Popeye nodded.

He couldn't believe he had left Boo back in the woods all by himself like that.

He felt like a bad person.

A real bad person.

There wasn't a word in the dictionary bad enough to describe him.

callous: *adjective*; having an insensitive and cruel disregard for others

No.
Worse than that.

abhorrent: *adjective*; inspiring disgust and loathing

No.
Worse than that.

There just wasn't a word.

"Okay," Elvis said, rubbing his palms together and peering out from under his shaggy hair in that solemn way of his. Then he slapped Popeye on the back and said, "Good luck."

Popeye walked over to Velma, his heart pounding, his face already feeling flushed with guilt.

"Um, Velma?" he said, keeping his voice low so Calvin and them couldn't hear.

Velma kept her eyes on Dooley and Shifty, who were struggling to get the jack up under the motor home.

"Boo's back in the woods and me and Elvis are gonna go get him," Popeye said.

Velma's mouth was set in a thin, hard line.

"Okay?" Popeye stared down at his feet, the guilt stinging his face like fire ants.

Silence.

Popeye glanced up.

Velma was looking at him, her eyes narrowed into slits, her lips squeezed tight.

Popeye tried to make himself look like plain ole Popeye on the outside, but on the inside, he was feeling nothing but devious.

devious: *adjective*; showing a skillful use of underhanded tactics to achieve goals

underhanded: *adjective*; done in a dishonest way

"What's Boo doing back in the woods?" Velma said.

"I don't know."

That was not a lie.

"How do you know he's in the woods?" she said.

" 'Cause I saw him go in there."

That was not a lie.

"Why don't you just call him?"

"Well, um, he might not hear me."

That was not a lie.

Was it?

Velma flapped her arm out toward the woods. "All right," she said. "Go on. But you better get on back here as soon as you find him and don't be going too far. You hear me?"

"Yes, ma'am."

Well, he *did* hear her.

That was not a lie.

So Popeye turned and walked slowly back toward

Elvis, trying to look bored so Prissy and Calvin and them wouldn't notice.

Tra la la.

He made a sly little thumbs-up sign to Elvis and glanced over his shoulder. Prissy was doing cartwheels in the weeds. Walter and Willis were putting boards across the ditch. Calvin was wrestling with Shorty in the dirt.

Popeye and Elvis walked up the road, almost tiptoeing. But as soon as they got around the curve and out of sight of the motor home, they took off running to Popeye's house, around back, and through the field to the woods.

✳ ✳ ✳

Boo's tail swished back and forth in the dry leaves as Popeye untied the leash. "See?" he said. "I *told* you I wasn't going to be gone long." He took a piece of beef jerky from his pocket and held it out for Boo, who gobbled it up and swallowed it whole.

Popeye wiped his slobbery hand on his shorts. "Okay," he said to Elvis. "Let's go."

The two boys made their way along the creek with Boo trotting behind them. When they got to the

Indian pipes, they turned up the path to Starletta's.

Starletta's backyard was quiet. The chickens pecked at the dirt out by the garden.

"Maybe she's around front," Elvis said.

They ran around the side of the house.

The front yard was quiet. Yoo-hoo boats floated in the muddy water of the plastic swimming pool. The hose lay in a puddle beside it.

"Let's go knock on the back door," Elvis said.

Popeye's stomach did a little flip. "Her mom's liable to be in there," he said.

"So what?"

There it was again. That *So what?* that Elvis was so good at and Popeye was so bad at.

Popeye followed Elvis to the backyard and let out a sigh of relief when he saw Starletta hopping down the porch steps, wings aflapping.

Elvis didn't waste a minute. "Today's Wednesday," he said. "Show us the dead dogs."

Starletta looked him square in the eye and said, "No."

23

cajole: *verb*; to persuade someone to do
something by sustained coaxing or flattery

Popeye was not as good at cajoling as he was at
conniving.

But Elvis elbowed him and whispered, "You ask
her. She likes you better than me."

So Popeye was going to try his hand at cajoling.

"I bet you make the best Yoo-hoo boats in
Fayette," he said.

That was the flattery part of cajoling.

"Shoot, I bet you make the best Yoo-hoo boats in

the whole state of South Carolina," he said to Starletta.

That was adding more flattery to the cajoling in case the first flattery wasn't enough.

Starletta did not look particularly flattered.

She tossed some rocks into a rusty metal wagon and said, "Wanna help me build a monument?"

Popeye looked at Elvis, who gave a little nod and made some faces like he was sending Popeye a secret signal.

"Um, a monument?" Popeye said. "What kind of monument?"

Starletta tossed another rock into the wagon with a clang. "Just a plain ole monument," she said.

"Uh, sure."

So Popeye and Elvis helped Starletta gather rocks, filling the wagon until the rocks began to tumble over the sides and the wagon was so heavy all three of them together could hardly pull it.

Boo sat in the shade under the porch steps, snapping at the gnats that flitted around his droopy eyes.

While Popeye looked for rocks with Starletta, he

worked on the sustained coaxing part of cajoling.

He asked her where the dead dogs lived. (Three times.)

He reminded her that today was Wednesday. (Twice.)

He told her that Dooley and Shifty were digging out the Holiday Rambler right this very minute so Elvis would be leaving any time now.

But nothing worked.

Starletta just kept looking for rocks and digging up rocks and carrying rocks over to the wagon without saying a single word.

Elvis looked like he was about to bust wide open. His face was red and his fingers clenched into fists until his knuckles turned white. He kicked at dirt and puffed his cheeks out and let go with big, sputtering sighs that blew his hair up off his forehead.

Popeye was starting to think that he would never get the hang of cajoling.

But then he got an idea.

"Hey, Starletta," he said. "If you show us where the dead dogs live, you can ride in the Holiday Rambler."

Starletta froze, holding a dirty rock over the wagon with both hands. "Really?"

"Yep." Popeye nodded. "Right, Elvis?"

Elvis's face lit up. "Sure!"

Starletta dropped the rock into the wagon and raced toward the garden calling, "Come on!"

24

POPEYE'S INSIDES WERE SWIRLING in a yippee kind of way as he raced around the garden and into the woods with Elvis and Boo, following Starletta to the dead dog place. A thick layer of rotting leaves and clumps of moss carpeted the narrow path that zigged and zagged and zigged some more. From somewhere through the trees came the faint, water-flowing sound of the creek. Popeye and Elvis and Boo hurried to keep up with Starletta as they jumped over logs and pushed aside branches.

And then . . .

. . . the path ended.

The sky was suddenly open and bright above them, no longer hidden by the thick, overhanging branches of the trees. Boulders and tree stumps and dense, overgrown shrubs lined the edges of the clearing. On the far side, a gravel road disappeared over the slope of a weed-covered hill.

Starletta threw her arms out and said, "Ta da!"

Scattered around the clearing, nestled among the weeds and wildflowers, were grave markers.

Some of them were stone.

Some of them were wood.

Some of them were old and crumbling and falling over.

Some of them were shiny and clean and standing straight.

And some of them had pictures on them.

Pictures of dogs.

"See?" Starletta said. "Dead dogs."

A dog cemetery!

Popeye was dumbstruck.

dumbstruck: *adjective*; so shocked or surprised as to be unable to speak

Starletta pointed to a sign nailed to a tree at the edge of the cemetery:

ONLY CEMETERY OF ITS KIND
IN THE WORLD;
ONLY COONHOUNDS ARE ALLOWED
TO BE BURIED HERE

"What are coonhounds?" Elvis said.

"Hunting dogs," Starletta said. "They hunt raccoons." She pointed to a tall stone monument surrounded by a rickety wooden fence in the middle of the cemetery. "That's where Troop is buried."

A sign at the base of the monument read:

TROOP
FIRST DOG LAID TO REST HERE
SEPTEMBER 4, 1937

Popeye walked around the cemetery, studying each of the graves, reading about the dogs who were buried there.

BIG ROY
FAITHFUL FRIEND
DIED 1976
AGE 14

BEAR
BORN AUG. 1, 1965
DIED OCT. 9, 1971
BELOVED COMPANION OF
HARLEY T. JANSON

KATE
GONE BUT NOT FORGOTTEN
1978–1990

OLD BLUE
HE WAS AS GOOD AS THE BEST
AND BETTER THAN THE REST
1953–1965

Most of the graves had vases or soda bottles holding colorful plastic flowers. One grave had a little plastic raccoon sitting on top of a crumbling stone etched with the name Loud.

Some of the graves had been carefully tended. Others were overgrown and long forgotten.

Popeye studied the photos sealed in plastic and taped on the stone markers or nailed to pieces of wood.

A man in a hunting cap kneeling in a field with his arm around a black and tan dog.

A long-eared brown and white dog panting in the back of a pickup truck, one paw resting in the lap of a bearded man in overalls.

Much-loved dogs.

Like Boo.

Elvis darted from one grave to another saying, "Cool!" and "Look at this one!"

Starletta skipped around the cemetery, reciting the dog names on all the graves she passed. "Bubba Dog, Old Blue, Tater . . ." The sequined edges of her butterfly wings glittered in the sun.

Popeye was still dumbstruck.

He had lived on the gravel road in Fayette, South Carolina, his whole life and had never dreamed that on the other side of the woods behind his house, just beyond the creek where he had played a million times, was a cemetery full of dead dogs. A place where grown men left flowers in soda bottles and called their dogs *beloved*.

Popeye took a deep breath, the sweet scent of honeysuckle tickling his nose.

He wanted to savor this moment.

savor: *verb*; to enjoy or appreciate completely

So while Elvis darted and Starletta skipped, Popeye savored.

Until Velma stepped out of the woods.

25

VELMA'S APPEARANCE at the edge of the cemetery, arms crossed, face red, was definitely not
serendipity. It was much closer to vicissitude. Her
livid wrath was like sparks, shooting from grave to
grave, from tree to shrub, from Popeye to Elvis.

Popeye wished he hadn't connived and cajoled.
He should have listened to his qualms. Then maybe
he wouldn't have been standing here all shamefaced
in the middle of a coonhound cemetery beside a girl
with butterfly wings and Elvis with his so-what?
face.

Velma stomped over to Popeye and gave him a little whack on the arm when she asked him what in

the world had gotten into him. Then another whack when she asked him if he had plumb lost his mind. And another whack when she told him she'd been traipsing through the woods for an hour looking for him. And one last whack when she asked him if he was trying to worry her right into the grave.

Then she spun around and glared at Elvis. "And you!" she hollered, jabbing her finger at him.

She lit into Elvis while he peered up at her from under his shaggy hair. As she hollered on and on about how he oughta be over there helping with that motor home and nobody even knew where he was and did he want to grow up to be like Dooley and Shifty and all those other no-accounts, his so-what? face began to change. By the time she was done with him, he was wearing a pretty good I'm-sorry face.

Then the quiet drifted down and hovered over them until Starletta shattered it like glass.

"These are all dead dogs," she said, throwing her arms out. "And they live here." She pointed to each grave, reading off the dog names like she was taking roll. "Jasper, Connie, Big Tick, Rollo . . ."

"Who are you?" Velma interrupted.

"Princess Starletta Rainey."

"Rainey?" Velma's eyes narrowed. "Where do you live?"

Starletta pointed toward the woods.

Velma looked over at the path that zigzagged through the trees. "Is your daddy T-Bone Rainey?"

Starletta skipped in a circle around one of the graves.

JAY BOB
BEST DOG EVER
JUNE 16, 1955

"Yes, he is," she said.

"I know him," Velma said. "His daddy used to deliver firewood to me when he wasn't no bigger than you."

Starletta kept skipping, not even looking at Velma.

Popeye felt the wrath-filled air swirling around Velma.

"I *know*," Velma snapped, "that your daddy would not approve of three younguns running wild and unsupervised in these woods."

Starletta stopped skipping and thrust her chin up. "That is most definitely *not* true," she said.

Popeye's insides danced with delight at little ole butterfly-winged Starletta standing up to Velma, something he had never done in all his born days and never intended to do, not even when he was old.

Velma's face twitched. Her hand fluttered up and pushed at her thin gray hair. Popeye could tell that all she wanted to do in the whole world, at that moment, was find herself a rolled-up newspaper and swat Starletta's skinny legs.

But, of course, she couldn't.

So she turned to Popeye and said, "Let's go."

26

THEY TRUDGED SILENTLY down the path in
single file.

Popeye, Elvis, Boo, and Velma.

Starletta skipped along behind them, humming.

Every now and then, Velma whirled around
and told her to go on home, but Starletta ignored
her.

They turned left at the Indian pipes and followed
the creek until they got to the dam the boys had
made. By the time they reached the field behind
Popeye's house, they could hear the folks up at the
Holiday Rambler.

"A little more to the left!"

"Give her some gas!"

"On the count of three . . ."

And then, just as they rounded the curve, the Holiday Rambler drove out of the hole in the road with a roar, sending up swirls of dirt and gravel.

A cheer rose into the warm summer air.

Prissy, Calvin, Walter, Willis, and Shorty whooped and clapped.

Dooley and Shifty high-fived each other.

Glory and Furman Jewell grinned down at everyone from the window of the motor home.

Elvis yelled, "Hot dang!" and ran over to join the others.

Velma nodded at Dooley with the teeny-tiniest little smile at the corners of her thin lips.

Starletta skipped over to the motor home, her wings flapping so much it was a wonder she didn't lift right up into the sky like a bird.

It seemed like everybody was just as happy as happy could be.

Everybody except Popeye.

When Popeye saw the shiny silver motor home drive out of the hole in the road, a wave of melancholy settled over him.

melancholy: *noun;* a deep sadness

If the motor home wasn't stuck anymore, then the motor home could drive away.

If the motor home *could* drive away, the motor home *would* drive away.

And Popeye would be left behind.

Left behind with nothing but the shed and the mailbox and the weeds and the ditch.

"Come on, y'all," Glory called from the window of the motor home. "Let's go for a ride."

When the door of the Holiday Rambler opened and everybody piled in (even Boo), Popeye's melancholy followed him like a rain cloud. He sat in the diner booth squished between Elvis and Calvin, across from Walter and Willis and Shorty. Velma and Dooley and Shifty sat on the fold-down bed. Starletta and Prissy hopped around in circles, holding hands and giggling until Glory told them to sit down and behave.

Then the motor home began to move. It bounced and squeaked and rumbled up the gravel road, but when it turned onto the main highway, it settled into a steady purr. A warm breeze blew through the open windows, sending napkins and candy wrappers swirling around them.

As Popeye watched the road signs and telephone poles whiz by him from his seat in the diner booth, a little buzz of excitement began to stir inside him. He thought back to that day when the rain had left rivers of muddy water in the driveway and he had seen that tilted motor home gleaming in the morning sun for the first time. And now here he was, zooming up the highway in a silver dollhouse jammed with kids and paper plates and sneakers and notebooks full of country-western songs. Before long, Popeye's cloud of melancholy began to lift, higher and higher above him, until it drifted right out the window and disappeared into the Carolina sky.

When they got to the shopping center out by the interstate, Furman turned the motor home around and drove back toward Popeye's house. As they rumbled down the gravel road, Popeye looked out the window. There was his little house with the shed and the drainage ditch and the rusty trailer in the backyard. Tomorrow he would wake up to see the heart-shaped stain on the ceiling of his bedroom and

147

hear the *tick, tick, tick* of the clock in the living room.

Tomorrow, Velma would recite the kings and queens of England in chronological order and holler at Dooley.

Tomorrow, Boo would snore on his quilt by the woodstove.

Tomorrow, everything would be the same.

But different.

Because tomorrow, Popeye could reminisce.

reminisce: *verb*; to think about past events

He could reminisce about the Holiday Rambler with the howling coyote and the glittering lightning bolts.

Where would it be?

Zipping along a highway somewhere?

Bouncing up a gravel road?

He could reminisce about that passel of wild kids. Prissy and Calvin and Walter and Willis and Shorty—and most of all, Elvis.

What would they be doing?

Playing cards and eating sandwiches?

Jumping on the fold-down bed?

Fussing and fighting while Furman drove and Glory wrote country-western songs?

And tomorrow, Popeye could start his very own Spit and Swear Club (and he could be president).

Tomorrow, he would have a few great insults to use, if he needed them.

He could even be a Royal Rule Breaker, if he wanted to.

And long after the hole and the tire marks in the gravel road were gone, long after the summer wild-flowers had yellowed and died, when the mossy rocks were slippery with frost and the edges of the creek were crusted with a thin layer of winter ice, Popeye could look for the path where the Indian pipes had grown that summer. He could whistle for Boo to come with him to find Starletta, and the three of them could go visit the place where dead dogs live.

* * *

Popeye and Starletta sat on the big rock on the bank of the creek with Boo snoring beside them.

They unfolded and cut and unfolded and cut all afternoon.

After they had a whole pile of Yoo-hoo boats, Popeye tore a strip of notebook paper and wrote with a blue colored pencil:

The Small Adventure of Popeye and Elvis

He folded the strip of paper.

Once.

Twice.

Three times.

He tucked it inside one of the boats, then stepped down into the creek and set the boat on the water. He moved the branches and pushed aside the rocks and mud that he and Elvis had used to dam the water.

The little boat began to drift slowly down the creek. Before long, it picked up speed, dipping and bobbing in the flowing water. It bumped against rocks and slid over tiny waterfalls while minnows darted in curious circles around it.

Farther and farther it drifted, growing smaller and smaller, until it was a tiny yellow, brown, and blue dot that rounded the curve in the creek and disappeared.

Go Fish!

GOFISH

BARBARA O'CONNOR

What did you want to be when you grew up?
For most of my childhood, I wanted to be a teacher. I also thought I might like to be a dance instructor and have my own dancing school, which I actually did for a few years.

When did you realize you wanted to be a writer?
I don't remember ever making a conscious decision to be a writer. Writing was just something that I loved doing from a very young age. I still have boxes and boxes of things I wrote as a child, from poems to stories to plays.

What's your first childhood memory?
The earliest memory I have is when I was about four years old and the ice cream truck was coming through my neighborhood. My sister and all her friends were running after it but I couldn't keep up. I remember just standing there crying.

What's your favorite childhood memory?
Being at my grandmother's house in North Carolina with my cousins. My grandfather had filled an old chicken coop with

sand to make a huge indoor sandbox. We played in that chicken coop sandbox for hours.

As a young person, who did you look up to most?
My dad.

What was your worst subject in school?
Economics. (I'm still not very good at economics.)

What was your best subject in school?
English.

What was your first job?
I used to teach dancing lessons to neighborhood children. I had a dance studio in my garage that my father helped me make.

How did you celebrate publishing your first book?
With lots of whooping and yahooing—and then dinner out with my family.

Where do you write your books?
In the winter, I write in my office, which is a converted bedroom in my house. I have a huge, lovely desk that was handmade by a friend of mine. The wood is beautiful and there is lots of room for family photos. My two dogs always stay in there with me and keep me company.

In the summer, I love to sit out on my screened porch. I love being able to watch the birds and look at the flowers while I write.

Where do you find inspiration for your writing?
My biggest inspiration comes from my memories of my childhood in the South. But I also love to go back to the South and pay attention to all the little things that make it so special there: the

way the people talk and the food they eat; the weather; the trees—all the things that add richness to a story.

I'm also inspired by reading.

Which of your characters is most like you?
Jennalee in *Me and Rupert Goody*. I think I felt the most like her as I wrote her story and I definitely related to the setting of the Smoky Mountains, where I spent a lot of time as a child.

When you finish a book, who reads it first?
I belong to a writers group, so I share bits and pieces of my stories as I write them. But once the story is complete and polished, the first people who read it are my editor, Frances Foster, and my agent, Barbara Markowitz.

Are you a morning person or a night owl?
No question about it: a morning person!

What's your idea of the best meal ever?
Sushi! (But some good ole greasy fried chicken and big, hot, fluffy biscuits sound pretty good, too.)

Which do you like better: cats or dogs?
I am definitely an animal lover. I love them all. But dogs are my favorite. I adore them.

What do you value most in your friends?
A sense of humor, honesty, and respecting my need for "alone" time to recharge my batteries.

Where do you go for peace and quiet?
I like being home. But outside of my home, I love to walk with my dogs, either in the woods or at the beach.

What makes you laugh out loud?
My husband and son both have a great sense of humor, so I laugh with them a lot. My two dogs also make me laugh.

Who is your favorite fictional character?
Beverly Cleary's Ramona Quimby.

What are you most afraid of?
Heights and snakes.

What time of year do you like best?
Summer.

What's your favorite TV show?
Judge Judy.

If you were stranded on a desert island, who would you want for company?
Probably somebody who was very good at building boats out of things you find on a desert island.

If you could travel in time, where would you go?
The fifties. Everything seemed much simpler then.

What's the best advice you have ever received about writing?
Author Linda Sue Park often passes down advice that she got from Katherine Paterson, which is to set a goal of writing two pages a day. That doesn't seem nearly as daunting as sitting down to write a novel.

What do you want readers to remember about your books?

I'd like for readers to remember my characters, since that is the most important part of any story to me.

What would you do if you ever stopped writing?

I'd love to be a librarian, but it's probably too late, since I'd have to go back to school and I'm not sure I'm ready for that anymore. So, I guess I'd just stay home and play with my dogs and work in my garden and figure out a way to pay the electric bill.

What do you like best about yourself?

I'm very organized and always punctual. I also think I have a pretty good sense of humor.

What is your worst habit?

Always needing to plan things instead of being spontaneous. And, well, maybe nagging.

What do you consider to be your greatest accomplishment?

My greatest accomplishment is having raised a good son who is honest and kind. But I'm also pretty proud of having written books.

Where in the world do you feel most at home?

Down South.

What do you wish you could do better?

I wish I could sing and draw better. And I wish I could play a musical instrument.

What would your readers be most surprised to learn about you?

I have no sense of smell and I can eat a whole bag of cookies.

An amazing secret has just tumbled off a freight train in Carter, Georgia—and Owen is the only one who knows about it.

Keep reading for an excerpt from
THE FANTASTIC SECRET OF OWEN JESTER
by Barbara O'Connor

CHAPTER
ONE

Owen Jester tiptoed across the gleaming linoleum floor and slipped the frog into the soup.

It swam gracefully under the potatoes, pushing its froggy legs through the pale yellow broth. It circled the carrots and bumped into the celery and finally settled beside a parsnip, its bulging eyes staring unblinkingly up at Owen.

"See, Tooley? I told you," Owen said. "It's not hot."

He plucked a carrot out of the soup and popped it into his mouth.

Still cold.

Not yet heated up for his grandfather's supper.

Owen scurried into the pantry and hunkered down on the floor among the sacks of potatoes and jars of pickled okra and waited for Earlene.

When he heard the *clomp, clomp* of her heavy black shoes on the wooden stairs, he slapped a hand over his mouth to stifle a giggle. When he heard the kitchen door swing open, he slapped his other hand over his mouth, his shoulders shaking with a silent laugh. Then he peeked through the crack in the pantry door.

Earlene stomped over to the stove in that no-nonsense way of hers. She picked up a wooden spoon from the kitchen counter and peered into the pot. Then she placed the spoon back on the counter, stepped away from the stove, jammed both fists into her waist, and said, "Owen."

Her voice had that sharp edge to it that Owen had heard so many times before. He ducked back against the pantry wall and held his breath.

And then, quick as lightning, the pantry door burst open and Earlene's hand shot in, grabbed Owen by the collar, and yanked him to his feet.

Earlene was not a yeller.

Earlene was a snapper.

"Get that frog out of there," she snapped.

"You think that's funny?" she snapped.

She gave his collar a shake.

"You are a bad, bad child," she snapped. "And I thank my lucky stars every day that you are not mine."

She gave his collar another shake. "And I thank the good Lord up above that your grandfather doesn't know what's going on in this house."

She stomped over to the counter and began arranging pill bottles on a tray. "The very idea of that poor sick old man up there in the bed not able to do a thing but sleep and eat applesauce and you down here thinking up ways to make my life miserable."

Earlene sure knew how to ruin a good time.

After supper, Owen sat on his closet floor beside the plastic tub where Tooley lived and looked down at the frog. Tooley was the biggest, greenest, slimiest, most beautiful bullfrog ever to be seen in Carter, Georgia.

It had taken Owen nearly a month to catch him. A month of clomping through mud and scooping with fishnets and buckets and colanders and even a hamster cage. A month of squatting on logs, holding his breath, not moving a muscle, watching that big frog with the heart-shaped red spot between his bulging yellow eyes. A month of telling his friends Travis and Stumpy he was going to catch that frog no matter what.

And then one day, just last week, he did.

The right scoop with the right net at the right time.

He had brought the frog home and made him a perfect frog house in a plastic tub in the closet.

And he had named him Tooley Graham.

Tooley after his cousin who lived in Alabama and played in a rock-and-roll band and wore leather bracelets and made everyone mad when he came to Georgia to visit the family at Thanksgiving. (Everyone but Owen, who thought Tooley was cool.)

And Graham after the big pond where the bullfrog had lived before Owen caught him. Graham Pond.

Owen poked the frog with his finger. "Come on, Tooley," he said. "You gotta eat *something*."

But Tooley wouldn't even look at the dead fly that Owen had dropped into the water in the tub.

So Owen laid the chicken wire back on top of the tub, put a brick on top of the chicken wire, and flopped onto his bed, staring up at the ceiling. Travis and Stumpy were probably skateboarding over at the Bi-Lo parking lot. Maybe they were throwing rocks at the Quaker State Oil sign out on Highway 11. Or maybe they were thinking up some great new way to torture their dreaded enemy, Viola.

But Owen was stuck here in his bedroom, thanks to Earlene, who had tattled on him big-time as soon as his mother had gotten home from work. He could tell his mother had thought that soup trick was at least a little bit funny. He had seen the corners of her mouth twitch when Earlene went on and on about what a bad, bad boy he was.

But his mother had told his father and his father had slammed his fist on the kitchen table and hollered at Owen and now here he was in his bedroom, just him and Tooley.

Owen wished they had never moved in with his grandfather. He wished they still lived in that little house over on Tupelo Road. Travis had lived next door and Stumpy had lived across the street and life had been good.

But then the hardware store had closed and his father didn't have a job, so they had moved across town to live with his grandfather.

There were three good things and three bad things about living with his grandfather.

The three good things were:

1. There was a lot of land around the house, with woods and paths and sheds and the big pond where Tooley had lived.
2. There was a falling-down barn behind

the house that was filled with stuff, like a rusty unicycle and a crate full of horse-shoes and about a hundred rolls of chicken wire.

3. Train tracks ran behind the woods be-low the house, and every few days the whistle blew late at night as the train roared through Carter.

The three bad things were:

1. Earlene had been working for his grand-father for as long as Owen had been alive. Maybe longer. Earlene was grumpy and needed everything to be clean.

2. Travis and Stumpy lived farther away and sometimes did things without him.

3. Viola lived next door.

Owen did not like Viola.

There were a lot of reasons why he did not like Vi-ola, but the first four were:

1. Viola was nosy.

2. Viola was bossy.

3. Viola wore glasses that made her eyes look big, like a fly's.

4. Viola was a know-it-all.

There was only one good thing about Viola:

She had allergies.

Viola was allergic to pine and grass and dust and dogs and just about every good thing in life.

This was a good thing because it meant that Viola didn't like to play in the woods or the fields or down by the pond. And she never went inside Owen's grandfather's house, where Owen's dogs, Pete and Leroy, left tumbleweeds of fur along the baseboards of every room.

Owen checked on Tooley one more time before he turned off the lamp beside the bed. Then he sat by the window and took a deep breath of the summer night air. It smelled like pine and grass and honeysuckle.

Far off in the distance, the train whistle blew. Owen waited, listening for the faint clatter of the train on the tracks to get louder and louder as it got closer to Carter.

In a blink, the train was whooshing down the tracks behind the house.

Clatter, clatter, clatter.

And then . . . something else.

A noise Owen had never heard before.

From way down by the tracks.

A thud.

The crack of wood.

A tumble, tumble, tumble sound.

Then the *clatter, clatter, clatter* of the train grew fainter and fainter until the only sound left was the chirp of the crickets in the garden beneath the window.

IF YOU LIKE ANIMALS, YOU'LL LOVE THESE DOG TALES AVAILABLE FROM SQUARE FISH

Dog Whisperer: The Rescue
Nicholas Edwards
ISBN-13: 978-0-312-36768-8
$6.99 US / $7.99 Can

An adopted girl, an
abandoned dog—together,
they can save others.

How to Steal a Dog
Barbara O'Connor
ISBN-13: 978-0-312-56112-3
$6.99 US / $7.99 Can

Georgina may soon be
homeless, but a missing dog
poster has just given her hope!

Dog Gone
Cynthia Chapman Willis
ISBN-13: 978-0-312-56113-0
$6.99 US / $7.99 Can

When searching for her runaway dog,
young Dill must also deal with the
death of her mother, and her
father's grief.

It Only Looks Easy
Pamela Curtis Swallow
ISBN-13: 978-0-312-56114-7
$6.99 US / $7.99 Can

Do desperate times always call
for desperate measures?

Lunchbox and the Aliens
Bryan W. Fields
ISBN-13: 978-0-312-56115-4
$6.99 US / $7.99 Can

Beware—the fate of the world
rests in the paws of a
basset hound and a pair of
clueless aliens!

Sheep
Valerie Hobbs
ISBN-13: 978-0-312-56116-1
$6.99 US / $7.99 Can

Will this dog ever find a boy or
a place to call home?

SQUARE FISH
WWW.SQUAREFISHBOOKS.COM
AVAILABLE WHEREVER BOOKS ARE SOLD